Praise for *The Boy in the Dress*

"well written, funny, touching" *Observer*

"Charming, funny, with lovely illustrations from Quentin Blake" *The Times*

"A great and comic tale – Walliams is a natural wit and good with words" *Evening Standard*

"Walliams's storytelling has a lovely Dahlian fluency to it" *Time Out*

"The Little Britain star's debut novel is a passionate celebration of individuality" *Telegraph*

"I was surprised by how tender and kind Walliams's first book for children is... a touching story" *Independent on Sunday*

"Believable characters and a story that's original and intriguing: *****" *Heat Magazine*

"has an old-fashioned, spiky morality that those of us who grew up on Roald Dahl know and love" *Observer Woman*

"Charming, surprising and hilarious – everything you would expect from David Walliams: ****" *Look Magazine*

"Hilariously funny – just as you'd expect!" *Mizz*

David Walliams

The
Boy in
the Dress

Illustrated by Quentin Blake

HarperCollins *Children's Books*

First published in hardback in Great Britain by HarperCollins
Children's Books 2008
First published in paperback in Great Britain by HarperCollins
Children's Books 2009
HarperCollins *Children's Books* is a division of
HarperCollinsPublishers Ltd
77–85 Fulham Palace Road, Hammersmith, London W6 8JB

The HarperCollins website address is:
www.harpercollins.co.uk

14

Text © David Walliams 2008
Illustrations © Quentin Blake 2008

David Walliams and Quentin Blake assert the moral right to be
identified as the author and illustrator of this work

ISBN 978-0-00-727904-3

Printed and bound in England by
Clays Ltd, St Ives plc

For Eddie,

What joy you have given us all.

1

No Hugging

Dennis was different.

When he looked in the mirror he saw an ordinary twelve-year-old boy. But he *felt* different – his thoughts were full of colour and poetry, though his life could be very boring.

The story I am going to tell you begins here, in Dennis's ordinary house on an ordinary street in an ordinary town. His house was nearly exactly the same as all the others in the street. One house had double glazing, another did not. One had a gravel drive, another had crazy paving. One had a Vauxhall Cavalier in the drive, another a Vauxhall Astra. Tiny differences that only really pointed out the sameness of everything.

It was all so ordinary, something extraordinary just had to happen.

Dennis lived with his dad – who did have a name, but Dennis just called him Dad, so I will too – and his older brother John, who was fourteen. Dennis found it frustrating that his brother would always be two years older than him, and bigger, and stronger.

Dennis's mum had left home a couple of years ago. Before that, Dennis used to creep out of his room and sit at the top of the stairs and listen to his mum and dad shout at each other until one day the shouting stopped.

She was gone.

Dad banned John and Dennis from ever mentioning Mum again. And soon after she left, he went around the house and took down all the photographs of her and burnt them in a big bonfire.

But Dennis managed to save one.

One solitary photograph escaped the flames, dancing up into the air from the heat of the fire, before floating through the smoke and onto the hedge.

As dusk fell, Dennis snuck out and retrieved the photo. It was charred and blackened around the edges and at first his heart sank, but when he turned it to the light he saw that the image was as bright and clear as ever.

It showed a joyful scene: a younger John and Dennis with Mum at the beach, Mum wearing a lovely yellow dress with flowers on it. Dennis loved that dress; it was full of colour and life, and soft to the touch. When Mum put it on it meant that summer had arrived.

It had been warm outside after she had left, but it hadn't really been summer in their house again.

In the picture Dennis and his brother were in swimming trunks holding ice-cream cones, vanilla ice-cream smeared around their smiling mouths. Dennis kept the photo in his pocket and looked at it secretly every day. His mum looked so achingly beautiful in it, even though her smile was uncertain. Dennis stared at it for hours on end, trying to imagine what she had been thinking when it was taken.

After Mum left, Dad didn't say much, but when he did, he would often shout. So Dennis ended up watching a lot of television, and especially his favourite show, *Trisha*. Dennis had seen a *Trisha* episode about people with depression, and thought maybe his dad had that. Dennis loved *Trisha*. It was a daytime talk show where ordinary people were given the opportunity to talk about their problems, or yell abuse at their relatives, and it was all presided over by a kindly looking but judgemental woman conveniently called... Trisha.

For a while Dennis thought life without his mum would be some kind of adventure. He'd stay up late, eat take-aways and watch rude comedy shows. However, as the days turned into weeks, and the weeks turned into months, and the months turned into years, he realised that it wasn't an adventure at all.

It was just sad.

Dennis and John sort of loved each other in that way that they had to because they were brothers. But John tested this love quite often by doing things he thought were funny, like sitting on Dennis's face and farting. If farting had been an Olympic sport (at time of writing I am told it isn't, which I feel is a shame), he would have won a number of gold medals and probably received a knighthood from the Queen.

Now, reader, you might be thinking that as their mum had left, the two brothers would be brought closer together.

Sadly, it only drove them apart.

Unlike Dennis, John was full of silent rage with his mum for leaving, and agreed with Dad that it was better never to mention her again. It was one of the rules of the house:

No talking about Mum.

No crying.

And worst of all – no hugging.

Dennis, on the other hand, was just full of sadness. Sometimes he missed his mum so much that he cried in bed at night. He tried to cry as quietly as possible, because he and his brother shared a room and he didn't want John to hear.

But one night Dennis's sobs woke John up.

"Dennis? Dennis? What are you crying for now?" demanded John from his bed.

"I don't know. It's just… well… I just wish that Mum was here, and everything," came the reply from Dennis.

"Well, don't cry. She's gone and she's not coming back."

"You don't know that…"

"She's never coming back, Dennis. Now stop crying. Only girls cry."

But Dennis *couldn't* stop crying. The pain ebbed and flowed inside him like the sea, crashing down on him, almost drowning him in tears. He didn't want to upset his brother, though, so he cried as quietly as he possibly could.

So why was Dennis so different, I hear you ask? After all, this boy lived in an ordinary house, in an ordinary street, in an ordinary town.

Well, I'm not going to tell you why yet, but the clue might be in the title of this book…

2

Fat Dad

Dennis's dad jumped up and down and shouted with joy. Then he pulled Dennis into a tight hug.

"Two nil!" he said. "We showed 'em, eh son?"

Yes, I know I said there was no hugging in Dennis's house. But this was different.

It was football.

In Dennis's house talking about football was easier than talking about feelings. He, John and Dad all loved football, and together shared the highs and (more often) lows of supporting their local third-division team.

But as soon as the match finished and the referee blew his whistle, it was as if that sound also signalled a return to their strict no-hugging policy.

Dennis did miss being hugged. His mum had hugged him all the time. She was so warm and soft, he loved being held by her. Most children can't wait to grow up and get bigger, but Dennis missed being small and being picked up by his mother. It was in her arms that he had felt most safe.

It was a shame Dennis's dad hardly ever hugged him. Fat people are good at hugs, they're nice and soft, like a big comfy sofa.

Oh, yes, didn't I mention? Dad was fat.

Really fat.

Dad worked as a long-distance lorry driver. And all that sitting down and driving had taken its toll, only stretching his legs to go to the

service station café and eat various combinations
of eggs, sausage, bacon, beans and chips.

Sometimes, after breakfast, Dad would eat
two packets of crisps. He just got fatter and
fatter after Mum left. Dennis had seen a *Trisha*
episode about a man called Barry who was so
fat he couldn't wipe his own bum. The studio
audience were told about his daily food intake

and "oohed" and "aahed" with a strange mixture of delight and horror. Then Trisha asked him, "Barry, does the fact that you have to get your mum or dad to wipe your… underneath… not make you want to lose weight?"

"Trisha, I just love me food," was Barry's smirking reply.

Trisha put it to Barry that he was "comfort

eating". Trisha was good with phrases like that. She had after all been through a lot of difficult times herself. Barry cried a bit at the end, and as the credits rolled Trisha smiled sadly and gave him a hug, though it was hard for her to really get her arms around Barry as he was the size of a small bungalow.

Dennis wondered whether his dad was comfort eating too, having one more sausage or slice of fried bread at breakfast to – in Trisha's words – "fill the emptiness inside". But he didn't dare share that thought with his dad. Dad wasn't keen on Dennis watching the show anyway. He said, "It's just for girls, that."

Dennis dreamed of one day having his own *Trisha* episode, with the title, "My brother's farts smell well bad" or "My dad has a chocolate Hob-Nob problem". (Dad ate a whole packet of the admittedly more-ish biscuits every day when he got home from work.)

So when Dennis, his dad and John played football, Dad would always go in goal, because he was so fat. He liked it because it meant he didn't have to run around that much. The goal was an upturned bucket and an empty beer keg, a remnant from a long-forgotten barbecue they'd once had when Mum was still around.

They didn't have barbecues any more. These days they had battered sausages from the local chippy, or bowls of cereal, even when it wasn't breakfast.

What Dennis loved most about playing football with his family was that he was the best. Even though his brother was two years older, Dennis could run rings around him in the garden, tackling, dribbling, and scoring with great skill. And it wasn't like it was *easy* to get

the ball past his dad. Not because Dad was good
in goal – it was just that he was so *big*...

On Sunday mornings Dennis used to play
football for his local club. He dreamed of being
a professional footballer, but after his mum and
dad split up he stopped going. He had always

relied on his mum to give him a lift – Dad couldn't take him as he was forever driving up and down the country in his lorry trying to make ends meet.

So Dennis's dream floated quietly away.

Dennis did play football for his school

though, and was his team's number one...
shooter?

Sorry, reader, I must look this up.

Ah, *striker*.

Yes, Dennis was his team's number one
striker, scoring over a million goals in a year.

Excuse me again, reader, I don't know much
about football, maybe a million is too much. A
thousand? A hundred? Two?

Whatever, he scored the most goals.

As a result, Dennis was incredibly popular
with his team-mates – except the captain,
Gareth, who picked Dennis up on every little
mistake on the pitch. Dennis suspected that
Gareth was jealous of him because he was a
better footballer. Gareth was one of those boys
who are unusually large for their age. In fact
you wouldn't be surprised to find he was really
five years older than everyone else in his year,

but had just been held back on account of being a bit thick.

Once, Dennis was off school with a really bad cold on a match day. He had just finished watching that day's *Trisha*, a gripping episode about a woman who discovered she was having an affair with her own husband. Then he was looking forward to some Heinz tomato soup and his second favourite show *Loose Women*, where a panel of angry looking ladies debated important issues of the day – like diets and leggings.

But just as the signature tune was starting there was a knock at the door. Dennis got up grumpily. It was Darvesh, Dennis's best friend at school.

"Dennis, we desperately need you to play today," pleaded Darvesh.

"I'm sorry, Darvesh, I'm just not feeling well.

I can't stop sneezing or coughing. Aaachoooo! See?" replied Dennis.

"But it's the quarter finals today. We've always got knocked out at the quarter-finals before. Please?"

Dennis sneezed again.

"Aaaaaaaaaaaaaaaaaaaccccccccccchhhhh hhhhhoooooooooooooooOOO!" It was such a strong sneeze he thought he was going to turn inside out.

"Pleeeaaassseee," said Darvesh hopefully as he discreetly wiped some of Dennis's stray snot from his tie.

"OK, I'll try," coughed Dennis.

"Yeeeessss!" exclaimed Darvesh, as if victory was already theirs.

Dennis gulped down a couple of mouthfuls of soup, grabbed his kit and ran out of the house.

Darvesh's mum was sitting in her little red

Ford Fiesta outside, with the engine running. She worked on the tills at Sainsbury's, but lived to see her son play football. She was the proudest mum in the world, which always made her son squirm a little.

"Thank goodness you have come, Dennis!" she said as Dennis clambered onto the back seat. "The team needs you today, it's a very important match. Without doubt the most important match of the season!"

"Just drive please, Mum!" said Darvesh.

"All right! All right! We're going! Don't talk to your mother like that Darvesh!" she shouted, pretending to be angrier than she really was. She put her foot on the accelerator and the car lurched uncertainly off towards the school playing fields.

"Oh, you've decided to come have you?" growled Gareth as they pulled up. Not only was he bigger than everyone else, he had a deeper voice, and was disturbingly hairy for a boy his age. When he showered he looked like a big monkey.

"Sorry, Gareth I just wasn't feeling well. I have a pretty bad…"

Before Dennis could say "cold", he sneezed again even more violently than before.

"Aaaaaaaaaaaaaaaaaaaaaaaaaaaaaaaaaaaaaaaaaaaaaa
aaaaaaaaaaaaaaaaaaaaaaaaaaaaacccccccc
ccccccccccccccccccccccccccchccccc
cchhhhhhhhhhhhhhhhhhhhhhh
hhhhhhhooooooooooooooooooo
oooooooooooOOOOOO!"

"Oh sorry, Gareth," said Dennis, wiping a small gloop of snot from Gareth's ear with a tissue.

"Let's just do this," said Gareth.

Feeling weak with illness, Dennis ran onto the school pitch with his team, coughing and spluttering all the way.

"Good luck boys! Especially my son Darvesh, and of course his friend Dennis! Let's win this for the school!" shouted Darvesh's mum from the side of the pitch.

"My mum is like so embarrassing," rumbled Darvesh.

"I think it's cool she comes," said Dennis. "My dad's never seen me playing in a match."

"Let's see a nice goal from you today please, Darvesh my son!"

"Mmm, maybe she *is* a bit embarrassing," agreed Dennis.

That afternoon they were playing St Kenneth's School for Boys, one of those schools where the pupils felt a little superior just because their parents had to pay for them to go there. They were a very good team though, and within the first ten minutes had scored. The pressure was immediately on, and Darvesh stole the ball off a boy who looked twice his size and passed it to Dennis.

"Lovely tackle, Darvesh my son!" shouted Darvesh's mum.

The thrill of possessing the ball made Dennis forget his cold for a moment, and he weaved his way through the defence and approached the goal-keeper, a luxuriant-haired boy sporting brand new kit, who was probably called Oscar or Tobias or something. All of a sudden they were face to face, and Dennis sneezed again uncontrollably.

"Aaaaaaaaaaaaaccccccccccchhhhhhhh
hhhoooooooooooooOOO!!!!"

The snot exploded onto the goalie's face,
blinding him for a moment, and all Dennis
needed to do was tap the ball past the line.

"Foul!" shouted the goal-keeper, but the referee
allowed it. It was foul, but not technically *a* foul.

"I'm sorry about that," said Dennis. He really
hadn't meant to do it.

"Don't worry, I have a tissue!" exclaimed
Darvesh's mum. "I always carry a packet
with me." She hurtled onto the pitch, hitching
up her sari to avoid the mud and ran up to the
goalie. "There you go, posh boy," she said,
handing him the tissue. Darvesh rolled his eyes
at his mother's one-woman pitch invasion. The
goalie tearfully wiped Dennis's mucus from his
floppy hair. "Personally I think St Kenneth's
doesn't stand a chance," she added.

"Mummmm!" shouted Darvesh.

"Sorry! Sorry! Play on!"

Four goals later, one from Dennis, one from Gareth, one from Darvesh, and one 'accidental' deflection from Darvesh's mum and the game was won.

"You are through to the semi-final boys! I can't wait!" exclaimed Darvesh's mum as she drove the boys home, beeping out tunes on the Ford Fiesta's horn in celebration. For her it was as if England had won the World Cup.

"Oh please don't come Mum, I beg you. Not if you're gonna do that again!"

"How dare you, Darvesh! You know I wouldn't miss the next game for the world. Oh you make me so proud!"

Darvesh and Dennis looked at each other and smiled. For a moment their victory on the pitch made them feel like they owned the Universe.

Even Dad raised a smile when Dennis told him that his team were through to the semi-finals.

But Dad wasn't going to stay happy for long...

3

Under the Mattress

"What the hell *is* this?" said Dad. His eyes were popping out, he was so angry.

"It's a magazine," replied Dennis.

"I can see it's a magazine."

Dennis wondered why his dad was asking, if he already knew what it was, but he kept that thought to himself.

"It's *Vogue* magazine, Dad."

"I can see it's *Vogue* magazine."

Dennis fell silent. He had bought the magazine from the newsagent's a few days before. Dennis liked the picture on the cover. It was of a very pretty girl in an even prettier yellow dress with what looked like roses sewn on the front, and it really reminded him of the dress his mum was wearing in the photograph he'd kept. He just had to buy it, even though the magazine was £3.80, and he only got £5 a week pocket money.

ONLY 17 SCHOOLCHILDREN ALLOWED IN AT ONE TIME read the sign in the newsagent's shop window. The shop was run by a very jolly man called Raj, who laughed even when nothing funny was happening. He laughed when he said your name as you walked through the door – and that was just what he did when Dennis went into the shop.

"Dennis! Ha ha!"

Seeing Raj laugh it was impossible not to laugh too. Dennis visited Raj's shop most days on his way to or from school, sometimes just to chat to Raj, and after he picked up the copy of *Vogue* he felt a twinge of embarrassment. He knew it was usually women who bought it, so he also picked up a copy of *Shoot* on the way to the counter, hoping to hide the *Vogue* underneath it. But after ringing up the *Shoot* magazine on the till, Raj paused.

He looked at the *Vogue* magazine, then at Dennis.

Dennis gulped.

"Are you sure you want this, Dennis?" asked Raj. "*Vogue* is mainly read by ladies, and your drama teacher Mr Howerd."

"Umm…" Dennis hesitated. "It's a present for a friend, Raj. It's her birthday."

"Oh, I see! Maybe you'd like some wrapping paper to go with it?"

"Um, OK." Dennis smiled. Raj was a wonderful businessman and very skilled at getting you to buy things you didn't really want.

"All the wrapping paper is over there by the greetings cards."

Dennis reluctantly wandered over.

"Oh!" said Raj, excited. "Maybe you need a card to go with it too! Let me help."

Raj bounded out from behind the counter and began to proudly show Dennis his range of cards. "These are very popular with the ladies. Flowers. Ladies love flowers." He pointed out another. "Kittens! Look at these lovely kittens. And PUPPIES!" Raj was really excited now. "Look at those lovely puppies! They're so beautiful, Dennis, that they make me want to cry."

"Er…" said Dennis, looking at the card with puppies on it, trying to understand why it might make someone shed actual tears.

"Does this lady friend of yours prefer kittens or puppies?" Raj asked.

"I'm not sure," said Dennis, unable to think what this "lady friend" of his might like, if she existed. "Puppies, I think, Raj."

"Puppies it is! These puppies are so beautiful I want to kiss them all over!"

Dennis tried to nod his head in agreement, but his head wouldn't move.

"Is this wrapping paper OK?" asked Raj, as he pulled out a roll of what looked suspiciously like unsold Christmas wrapping paper.

"It's got Father Christmas on it, Raj."

"Yes, Dennis, and he's wishing you a very happy birthday!" said Raj confidently.

"I think I'll just leave it, thanks."

"Buy one extra roll, I'll give you a third free," said Raj.

"No, thanks."

"Three rolls for the price of two! That's a very good offer!"

"No, thanks," said Dennis again.

"Seven rolls for the price of five?"

Dennis only got Ds in maths, so wasn't sure if

that was a better offer or not. But he didn't want seven rolls of Father Christmas wrapping paper, especially in March, so again he said, "No, thanks."

"Eleven rolls for the price of eight?"

"No, thanks."

"You're a madman, Dennis! That's three rolls free!"

"But I really don't need eleven rolls of wrapping paper," said Dennis.

"OK, OK," said Raj. "Let me just put these through the till for you."

Dennis followed Raj to the till. He glanced briefly at the sweets on the counter.

"*Vogue* magazine, *Shoot* magazine, card, and now you're eyeing up my Yorkie bars, aren't you?" said Raj, laughing.

"Well, I was just…"

"Take one."

"No, thanks."

"Take one," insisted Raj.

"It's OK."

"Please, Dennis, I want you to have a Yorkie bar."

"I don't really like Yorkie bars…"

"Everyone likes Yorkie bars! Please take one."

Dennis smiled and picked up a Yorkie.

"One Yorkie bar, sixty pence," said Raj.

Dennis's face dropped.

"So that's five pounds in total please," continued the shopkeeper.

Dennis rummaged in his pocket and pulled out some coins.

"As my favourite customer," said Raj, "I give you a discount."

"Oh, thank you," said Dennis.

"Four pounds and ninety-nine pence, please."

Dennis had walked halfway up the street before he heard a voice shout, "Sellotape!"

He looked round. Raj was holding a large box of Sellotape. "You need Sellotape to wrap the present!"

"No, thanks," said Dennis politely. "We've got some at home."

"Fifteen rolls for the price of thirteen!" Raj shouted.

Dennis smiled and carried on walking. He felt a sudden surge of excitement. He couldn't wait to get home and open the magazine, and gaze at its hundreds of glossy, colourful pages. He walked faster, then started jogging, and when he really couldn't contain his excitement any more he started running.

When he got home, Dennis bounded upstairs. He closed the bedroom door, lay down on his bed and turned the first page.

Like a treasure box from an old film, the magazine seemed to shine a golden light on his face. The first hundred pages were all adverts, but in a way they were the best bit – pages and pages of glorious photographs of beautiful women in beautiful clothes and make-up and jewellery and shoes and bags and sunglasses. Names like Yves Saint-Laurent, Christian Dior, Tom Ford, Alexander McQueen, Louis Vuitton, Marc Jacobs, and Stella McCartney ran underneath the images. Dennis didn't know who any of them were, but he loved the way their names looked on the page.

The adverts were followed by a few pages of writing – they looked boring so he didn't read them – then pages and pages of fashion shoots. These were not very different from the adverts, featuring more beautiful women in photographs that were moody and fabulous. The magazine even smelled exotic, as it had special pages where you pulled open a flap to have a sniff of the newest perfume. Dennis pored over every page, mesmerised by the dresses – their colour, their length, their cut. He could lose himself in the pages forever.

The glamour.

The beauty.

The perfection.

Suddenly he heard a key in the door. "Dennis? Oi, bro? Where are you?"

It was John.

Dennis quickly hid the magazine under his mattress. He knew somehow that he didn't want his brother to see it.

He opened the bedroom door and called down as innocently as he could from the top of the stairs. "I'm just up here."

"What are you doing?" asked John as he

leaped up the stairs, a Jaffa Cake in his mouth.

"Nothing. Just got home."

"Do you wanna have a kick about in the garden?"

"Yeah, OK."

But all the time they played, Dennis couldn't help thinking about the magazine. It was as if it was glowing like gold from under the mattress. That night when his brother was in the bath he quietly lifted the copy of *Vogue* from under the mattress and silently turned the pages, studying every hem, every stitch, every fabric.

Every moment he could, Dennis returned to this glorious world. It was his Narnia, only without the talking lion that's supposed to be Jesus.

But Dennis's escape to that magical world of glamour ended the day his dad discovered the magazine.

"I can see it's *Vogue*. What I want to know is why a son of mine wants to *look* at a fashion magazine?"

It sounded like a question, but there was such anger and force in Dad's voice Dennis wasn't sure if he really wanted an answer. Not that Dennis could think of one anyway.

"I just like it. It's only pictures and things about dresses and that."

"I can see that," said Dad, looking at the magazine.

And that was when he paused and a funny look crossed his face. He studied the cover for a moment – the girl in the flowery frock. "That dress. It's like the one your m—"

"Yes, Dad?"

"Nothing, Dennis. Nothing."

Dad looked for a moment like he was going to cry.

"It's OK, Dad," said Dennis softly, and he slowly moved his hand and placed it over his dad's. He remembered doing the same with his mum once when Dad had made her cry. He remembered how strange it felt too, a little boy comforting a grown-up.

Dad let Dennis hold his hand for a moment,

before moving it away, embarrassed. He raised his voice again. "No, son, it's just not right. Dresses. It's weird."

"Well, Dad, what are you doing looking under my mattress in the first place?"

In truth Dennis knew *exactly* why his dad was looking under his mattress. Dad owned a copy of a rude magazine like the ones on the top shelf at Raj's shop. Sometimes John would sneak into their dad's room and smuggle it out and look at it. Dennis looked at it too, sometimes, but didn't find it all that exciting. He was disappointed when the ladies took their clothes off – he preferred looking at what they were wearing.

Anyway, when John "borrowed" his father's magazine, it wasn't really like when you borrow a book from the library. There wasn't an inlay card that would have to be stamped by a bespectacled librarian, and you didn't incur fines if you returned it late.

So John usually just kept it.

Dennis guessed his dad's magazine had gone missing again, and he had been looking for it when he found the copy of *Vogue*.

"Well, I was just looking under your mattress because..." Dad looked uncomfortable, and then angry. "It doesn't matter why I was looking under your mattress. I'm your dad. I can look under your mattress any time I like!" He finished his speech with the tone of triumph grown-ups sometimes use when they are talking nonsense and they know it.

Dennis's dad brandished the magazine. "This is going in the dustbin, son."

"But Dad..." Dennis protested.

"I'm sorry. It's just not right. A boy your age reading *Vogue* magazine." He said "*Vogue* magazine" as if he was talking a foreign language he didn't understand. "It's just not right," he muttered over and over as he left the room.

Dennis sat on the edge of his bed. He listened as his dad clumped his way down the stairs, and then lifted the dustbin lid. Finally he heard a clanging *thud* as the magazine hit the bottom of the bin.

4

Wanting to Disappear

"Morning, Dennis, or should I say Denise!" said John, laughing cruelly.

"I told you not to mention it," said Dad sternly, as he coated his white toast with an inch thick layer of butter. When Mum was around she'd have made him have margarine.

And brown bread.

Dennis slumped down at the kitchen table in silence, not even looking at his brother. He poured himself some Rice Krispies.

"Seen any nice dresses recently?" taunted John. He laughed again.

"I told you to leave it alone!" said Dad, even louder than before.

"Magazines like that are for girls! And woofters!"

"SHUT UP!" said Dad.

Dennis suddenly didn't feel hungry any more, and picked up his bag and walked out of the door. He slammed it behind him. He could still hear Dad, saying, "What did I say, John? It's over, OK? It's in the bin."

Dennis walked unwillingly to school. He didn't want to be at home *or* at school. He was afraid his brother would tell somebody and he'd be laughed at. He just wanted to disappear. When he was much younger he used to believe that if he closed his eyes, no one else could see him.

Right now he wished it was true.

The first lesson of the day was history. Dennis

liked history – they were studying the Tudor dynasty, and he loved looking at the pictures of the kings and queens in all their finery. Especially Elizabeth I, who really knew how to "power dress", an expression he had read in *Vogue* next to a shoot of a model in a beautifully cut business suit. But Dennis always found chemistry – the next lesson – mind-numbingly boring. He spent most of the lesson staring at the periodic table, trying to fathom what it was.

When break-time came, Dennis played football as usual in the playground with his friends. He was having fun until he saw John with a group of his mates, the bad boys with short hair who the careers' advisors would probably advise to become nightclub bouncers or criminals. They ambled through the middle of the makeshift pitch.

Dennis held his breath.

John nodded at his brother, but said nothing.

Dennis let out a sigh of relief.

He was pretty sure his brother couldn't have told anyone that he'd bought a women's fashion magazine. After all, Darvesh was playing football with him as he always did. They played with an old tennis ball that Darvesh's dog Odd-Bod had chewed. It was a school rule that footballs weren't allowed in the playground in case a window got broken. Darvesh set Dennis up to score with a daring cross.

Then Dennis headed the ball and it flew too high up past what was meant to be the goal...

... and through the window of the headmaster's office.

John and his friends stared, mouths open. The playground fell silent.

You could have heard a pin drop, in the

unlikely event that someone had dropped a pin at that exact moment.

"Oops," said Darvesh.

"Yes, oops," said Dennis.

"Oops" was really an understatement. The headmaster, Mr Hawtrey, hated children. Actually, he hated everybody, probably even himself. He wore an immaculate three-piece grey suit, with a charcoal-coloured tie and dark-framed glasses. His hair was meticulously combed and parted, and he had a thin, black moustache. It was as if he actively wanted to look sinister. And he had a face that someone who has spent their whole life grimacing ends up with.

A permanently grimacing one.

"He might not be in his office," ventured Darvesh hopefully.

"Maybe," said Dennis, gulping.

At that moment the headmaster's face peered

out of the window. "SCHOOL!" he bellowed. The playground fell silent. "Who kicked this ball?" He held the tennis ball between his fingers with the same sense of disgust that dog owners do when they are forced to pick up their dog's doo-doo.

Dennis was too scared to say anything.

"I asked a question. WHO KICKED IT?"

Dennis gulped. "I didn't kick it, Sir," he offered tentatively. "But I *did* header it."

"Detention today, boy. Four o'clock."

"Thank you, Sir," said Dennis, not sure what else to say.

"Because of your behaviour all ball games in the playground are banned for today," added Mr Hawtrey before disappearing back into his study. A sigh of angry disappointment echoed around the playground. Dennis hated it when teachers did that, when they made everyone suffer to make you unpopular with your classmates. It was a cheap trick.

"Don't worry, Dennis," said Darvesh. "Everyone knows Mr Hawtrey's a total—"

"Yeah, I know."

They sat on their bags by the wall of the science block and opened their lunch boxes, devouring the sandwiches that were meant for lunch.

Dennis hadn't told Darvesh about buying *Vogue* – but he wanted to find out what his friend thought about it – in a roundabout way.

Darvesh was Sikh. As he was in the same year as Dennis and only twelve he didn't wear a turban yet. He wore a *patka*, a bobble-hat-type thing that kept his hair out of his face. That's because Sikh men aren't supposed to cut their hair. There were lots of different types of kids at the school, but Darvesh was the only one who wore a *patka*.

"Do *you* feel different Darvesh?" asked Dennis.

"In what way?"

"Well, just, you know, you're the only boy in school who has to wear one of those things on your head."

"Oh, that, yeah. Well, with my family of course I don't. And when Mum took me to India at Christmas to visit Grandma I didn't at all. All the Sikh boys were wearing them."

"But at school?"

"At first I did, yes. I felt a bit embarrassed 'cos I knew I looked different to everyone."

"Yeah."

"And then I suppose as people got to know me they realised I wasn't really that different. I just wear this funny thing on my head!" He laughed.

Dennis laughed too.

"Yeah, you're just my mate, Darvesh. I don't really think about the thing on your head at all. In fact, I'd quite like one."

"No, you wouldn't. It itches like hell! But you know, it would be boring if we were all the same wouldn't it?"

"It certainly would." Dennis smiled.

5

Just Doodling

Dennis had never had a detention before, so in a way he was quite looking forward to it. When he turned up at classroom 4C to report to the French teacher Miss Windsor, he noticed there was only one other person who had been sentenced to an hour's incarceration. It was Lisa.

Lisa James.

Only the most beautiful girl in the school.

She was super-cool too, and somehow she always made her school uniform look like it was a costume in a pop video. Even though they had never spoken Dennis had a really big crush on Lisa.

Not that anything would ever happen though – her being two years older and six inches taller made her literally out of reach.

"Hi," Lisa said. She had a gorgeous voice, rough round the edges but soft inside.

"Oh, hi, um…" Dennis pretended not to remember her name.

"Lisa. What's your name?"

Dennis thought for a moment about changing his name to something cooler like "Brad" or "Dirk" to try and impress her, but realised that would be insane.

"Dennis."

"Hi, Dennis," said Lisa. "What are you in for?"

"I headed a ball into Hawtrey's office."

"Cool!" said Lisa, laughing.

Dennis laughed a little too. She obviously assumed that he had headed the ball into the headmaster's office on purpose and he wasn't about to correct her.

"What about you?" asked Dennis.

"I wasn't 'wearing the correct school uniform'. This time Hawtrey said my skirt was too short."

Dennis looked down at Lisa's skirt. It *was* quite short.

"I don't care really," she continued. "I'd rather wear what I want and get the odd detention now and again."

"Sorry," interrupted Miss Windsor. "There's not really meant to be any talking in detention."

Miss Windsor was one of the nice teachers who didn't really enjoy telling pupils off. She would usually say "excuse me" or "sorry" before she did. She was probably in her late forties. Miss Windsor didn't wear a wedding ring or seem to have any kids. She liked to exude a little French sophistication, throwing colourful silk scarves over her shoulder with mock nonchalance, and devouring four-packs of croissants from the Tesco Metro at break-time.

"Sorry, Miss Windsor," said Lisa.

Dennis and Lisa smiled at each other. Dennis got back to his lines.

I must not header balls into the headmaster's window.
I must not header balls into the headmaster's window.
I must not header balls into the headmaster's window.

He looked over at what Lisa was doing. Instead of her lines, she was idly sketching some dress designs. A ball-gown with a plunging back

The Boy in the Dress

looked like it wouldn't be out of place in *Vogue*. She turned over the page and started sketching a strapless top and pencil skirt. Next to that she drew a long flowing white suit that went in and out in all the right places. Lisa clearly had a real flair for fashion.

"Excuse me," said Miss Windsor. "But you should really concentrate on your own work, Dennis."

"Sorry, Miss," said Dennis. He started his lines again.

I must not header balls into the headmaster's window.

I must not header vogue into the headmaster's window.

I must not read vogue into the headmaster's...

Dennis sighed and rubbed out the last few lines. He was getting distracted.

After about forty-five minutes, Miss Windsor looked at her watch anxiously and addressed the class of two.

"I'm sorry," she said, "but would either of you mind if we finished this detention fifteen minutes early? Only I would quite like to get home in time for *Neighbours*. Lassiter's coffee shop is re-opening today after the dramatic fire."

"No problem, Miss," said Lisa smiling. "Don't worry, we won't tell anyone!"

"Thank you," said Miss Windsor, confused for a moment that somehow the roles had been reversed, and it was Dennis and Lisa who were letting her off.

"Do you wanna walk me home, Dennis?" asked Lisa.

"What?" said Dennis, in a panic.

"I said, 'do you want to walk me home?'"

"Um, yeah, OK," said Dennis, trying to sound cool.

Dennis felt like a celebrity as he walked down the road with Lisa. He walked slowly so he could be with her for as long as possible.

"I couldn't help noticing your drawings. Those dress designs. They're brilliant," said Dennis.

"Oh thanks. They were nothing really, I was just doodling."

"And I love the way you look."

"Thank you," replied Lisa, trying not to laugh.

"I mean *dress*," Dennis corrected himself. "Dress, I love the way you dress."

"Thanks," said Lisa, smiling again. She looked so unutterably gorgeous when she smiled that Dennis could barely look at her. Instead he looked down at her shoes, noticing they were round-toed.

"Beautiful shoes," he offered.

"Well, thank you for noticing."

"Apparently round-toed shoes are in this year. Pointy-toed are out."

"Where did you read that?"

"*Vogue*. I mean…"

"You read *Vogue*?"

Dennis caught his breath. What had he said? In all the excitement of being with Lisa his tongue was running away with itself.

"Um… no… erm… well, yeah, once."

"I think that's cool."

"You *do*?" asked Dennis, incredulous.

"Yeah. Not nearly enough boys are into fashion."

"I suppose not…" Dennis said. He wasn't sure if he *was* into fashion, or just liked looking at pictures of pretty dresses, but he chose not to mention it.

"Do you have a favourite designer?" Lisa asked.

Dennis wasn't sure if he did, but he remembered really liking one of the dresses in the magazine, a cream floor-length ball-gown, designed by John Gally something.

"John Gally something," he said.

"John Galliano? Yeah, he's amazing. A legend. He designs all the pieces for Dior too."

Dennis loved that she said "pieces". That was the word they'd used in *Vogue* for items of clothes.

"Well, this is my house. Thanks, Dennis. Bye," said Lisa. Dennis's heart sank a little that their walk was already over. She went to go towards the front door, then stopped for a moment. "You could come over at the weekend if you like," she said. "I've got loads of great fashion magazines I could show you. I really want to be a designer or a stylist or something when I'm older."

"Well, you *are* very stylish," said Dennis. He meant it sincerely, but somehow it sounded cheesy.

"Thank you," said Lisa.

She knew she was.

Everyone knew she was.

"It's Saturday tomorrow. Is eleven o'clock any good for you?"

"Er… I think so," said Dennis. As if any event in his past or future could prevent him from being at her house at eleven.

"See you then," she said, as she gave him a smile and passed out of view.

And just like that, Dennis's world went back to normal again, like when the lights go on in the cinema at the end of a film.

6

Forever and a Moment

At 10:59am Dennis was waiting outside Lisa's house. She had said eleven o'clock, but he didn't want to seem too keen. So he waited for his watch to count the seconds until eleven.

54.

55.

56.

57.

58.

59.

00.

He pressed the bell. The faint sound of Lisa's

voice floated down the stairs, and the blurry vision of her through the glass of the door was enough to make his heart beat faster.

"Hey," she said, smiling.

"Hey," he said back. Not that he'd ever said "hey" to anyone before, but he wanted to be like Lisa.

"Come in," she said, and he followed her into the house. It was very similar to the one Dennis lived in, but where his was gloomy, Lisa's was full of light and colour. There were paintings and family pictures haphazardly arranged on the walls. A sweet smell of freshly baked cake lingered in the hall. "Do you want a drink?"

"A glass of white wine, perhaps?" said Dennis, trying to act three times his age.

Lisa looked bemused for a moment. "I don't have any wine. What else do you like?"

"Um Bongo."

Lisa raised her eyebrows. "I think we've got some Um Bongo."

She found a carton and poured a couple of glasses, then they went upstairs to her room.

Dennis instantly adored it. In truth it was how he would like his room to be. She had pictures from fashion magazines all over the walls, stylish shots of beautiful women, in glamorous locations. On the shelves were books about fashion or famous film stars like Audrey Hepburn or Marilyn Monroe. A sewing machine sat in the corner of the room and she had a big pile of *Vogue*s by the bed.

"I'm collecting them," she said. "I've got an Italian one too. It's hard to get here, but it's amazing. The best *Vogue* is Italian. Heavy though! Would you like to see it?"

"I'd love to," said Dennis. He'd had no idea there were different *Vogue*s around the world.

They sat on her bed together, slowly turning the pages. The first shoot was in colour, but featured dresses that were only black or white, or a combination of the two.

"Wow, that dress is gorgeous," said Dennis.

"Chanel. It's probably madly expensive, but it is beautiful."

"I love the sequins."

"And that slit up the side," said Lisa. She traced her fingers longingly along the page.

What seemed like forever and a moment went by, as they studied every page, discussing each detail of every dress. When they reached the end they felt like they'd been friends forever.

Lisa pulled out another magazine to show him one of her favourite shoots, or "stories" as she called them. It was from an old British *Vogue*, and featured lots of models in wigs and metallic dresses. It looked like a scene from an old science-fiction film. Dennis loved the extravagance of these fantasies, so different from the grey cold reality of his own life.

"You'd look stunning in that gold dress," said Dennis, pointing to a girl with similar hair colouring to Lisa.

"Anyone would. It's an amazing dress. I could never afford any of these, but I like to look at these pictures and get ideas for my own designs. Do you want to see?"

"Oh yeah!" replied Dennis excitedly.

Lisa pulled a large scrapbook from her shelf. It was full of brilliant illustrations she had drawn of skirts and blouses and dresses and hats. Next to these Lisa had stuck lots of things onto the page: strips of glittering fabric, cut-out photographs of film costumes, even buttons.

Dennis stopped Lisa turning the page at an especially gorgeous drawing she had done of an orange sequined dress.

"That one is *beautiful*," he said.

"Thanks, Dennis! I'm really pleased with it. I'm making it right now."

"Really? Can I see?"

"Of course."

She reached into her cupboard and pulled out the half-finished dress.

"I got this material really cheap. It was just from down the market," she said. "But I think it's going to look really good. It's a little bit 1970s, I think. Very glamorous."

She held up the dress by its hanger. Although it was still cut a little roughly around the edges, and had a few loose threads, it was covered in hundreds of little round sequins and twinkled effortlessly in the morning sunlight.

"It's amazing," said Dennis.

"It would look good on you!" said Lisa. She laughed and held the dress next to Dennis. He laughed too, and then looked down at it, allowing himself to imagine for a moment what he would look like wearing it, but then told himself to stop being silly.

"It's really beautiful," he said. "It's not fair though, is it? I mean boy's clothes are so boring."

"Well, I think all those rules are boring. About what people can and can't wear. Surely everyone should be able to wear whatever they like?"

"Yes, I suppose they should," said Dennis. He had never really been encouraged to think like this before. She was right. What was wrong with wearing the things you liked?

"Why don't you put it on?" Lisa asked with a cheeky smile.

There was silence for a moment.

"Maybe that's a crazy idea," Lisa said, back-tracking as she sensed Dennis's awkwardness. "But dresses can be beautiful, and dressing up is fun. I love putting on pretty dresses. I bet some boys would like it too. It's no big deal."

Dennis's heart was beating really fast – he wanted to say "yes", but he couldn't. He just couldn't. This was all a bit much...

"I've got to go," he snapped.

"Really?" asked Lisa, disappointed.

"Yes, I'm sorry, Lisa."

"Well, will you come and visit me again? Today has been really fun. The next issue of *Vogue* is out next week. Why don't you come over next Saturday?"

"I don't know…" said Dennis, as he rushed out of the house. "But thanks again for the Um Bongo."

7

Watching the Curtain Edges Grow Light

"Happy Birthday, Dad!" exclaimed Dennis and John excitedly.

"I don't like birthdays," said Dad.

Dennis's face fell. Sunday was always a miserable day for him. He knew that loads of families were sitting down together for a roast dinner, and that only made him think about Mum. When Dad did try and cook a Sunday roast for his sons, it only made their loss more painful. It was as if there was a place laid in all their minds for someone they loved who wasn't there.

And anyway, Dad was *not* a good cook.

But this Sunday was even worse than usual – it was Dad's birthday and he was determined not to celebrate it.

Dennis and John had waited all afternoon to wish him a happy birthday. He had left for work very early that day – now it was seven o'clock at night and Dad had just got in. The boys had crept downstairs to the kitchen to surprise him, where he was sitting alone wearing the same red-checked jacket he always did. He had a can of cheap lager and a bag of chips.

"Why don't you go and play, boys? I just want to be on my own."

The card and cake Dennis and John were holding seemed to fade away in their hands at Dad's words.

"I'm sorry, boys," he said, catching their hurt. "It's just there's not much to celebrate is there?"

"We got you a card, Dad, and a cake," offered John.

"Thanks." He opened the card. It was from Raj's shop and featured a big smiling cartoon bear inexplicably wearing sunglasses and Bermuda shorts. Dennis had chosen it from Raj's shop because it had "Happy Birthday to the Best Dad in the World" written on it.

"Thanks, boys," said Dad as he looked at it. "I don't deserve it though. I'm not the best dad in the world."

"Yes you are, Dad," said Dennis.

"*We* think you are," added John tentatively.

Dad stared at the card again. Dennis and John had thought it would make him happy, but it seemed to be having the opposite effect.

"I'm sorry, boys, it's just I find birthdays hard, you know, since your mum left."

"I know, Dad," said Dennis. John nodded and tried to smile.

"Dennis scored a goal today. For the school," said John, trying to change the subject to something happy.

"Did you, son?"

"Yes, Dad," said Dennis. "It was the semi-final today, and we won 2-1. I got one goal and Darvesh scored the other. We're through to the final."

"Well that's good," said Dad, staring into the distance. He took another gulp from his can. "Sorry. I just need to be alone for a bit."

"OK, Dad," said John, nodding to Dennis that they should leave. Dennis touched his dad's shoulder for a moment, before they retreated from the room. They had tried. But birthdays, Christmas, going on holiday, and even day trips to the sea – slowly all those things had disappeared. Mum had always organised them, and now they seemed a lifetime away. Home was becoming a very cold, grey place.

"I need a hug," said Dennis.

"I ain't hugging you."

"Why not?"

"I'm your brother. I ain't hugging you. It's weird. I've gotta go anyway. I told the boys I was gonna hang around on the wall outside the offy with them for a bit."

Dennis needed to get out of the house too. "I'm going to Darvesh's then. See you later."

As he walked across the park, he felt bad for leaving his dad on his own in the kitchen. He wished he could make Dad happy.

"What's up?" asked Darvesh, as they were looking at videos on YouTube in his bedroom.

"Nothing," said Dennis unconvincingly. He wasn't a good liar, but then lying is not a thing that it's good to be good at.

I, myself, have never ever lied.

Apart from just then.

"You seem, like, really distracted."

Dennis *was* distracted. Not only was he thinking about his dad, he couldn't stop thinking about that orange sequined dress.

"I'm sorry. Darvesh, you'd be my friend whatever wouldn't you?"

"Of course."

"Darvesh! Dennis! Would you boys like some refreshing Lucozade drink?" shouted Darvesh's mum from the next room.

"No thanks, Mum!" Darvesh shouted back, before sighing loudly. Dennis just smiled.

"It's a high energy beverage! It'll get your strength up for the final!" came the insistent reply.

"All right, Mum, maybe later!"

"Good boys! You'll make me very proud if you win. But you know I'll still be proud if you don't."

"Yes, yes…" said Darvesh. "She's so embarrassing."

"It's only because she loves you," said Dennis.

Darvesh went silent for a moment so Dennis changed the subject.

"Can I try on your hat thing?" he asked.

"My *patka*?"

"Yes your *patka*."

"Sure, if you really want. I've got a spare one here I think," said Darvesh as he rummaged in his drawer before pulling out another hat. He passed it to Dennis, and Dennis carefully put it on.

"How do I look?" asked Dennis.

"Like a bit of a prat!"

They both laughed loudly. Then Darvesh thought for a moment. "I mean, it doesn't make you Sikh, does it? On you it's just a hat. It's just dressing up, innit?"

Dennis walked home feeling a bit brighter. He'd even laughed at some of the stupid videos they'd found, particularly one of a cat clambering over a baby and putting its bum in the baby's face.

But when he walked in he saw that Dad was

still sitting at the kitchen table where they had left him, with another can of lager but the same cold and soggy chips.

"Hi, Dad," said Dennis, trying to sound happy to see him.

His dad looked up for a moment, and then sighed heavily.

John had already gone to bed. When Dennis went up, John didn't even bother saying anything. As they lay there the silence was deafening. There was nothing that could be said. Dennis couldn't sleep at all, and spent all night watching the curtain edges grow light.

Only one thing stopped him suffocating: thinking about Lisa, the world she had opened up for him, and that sequined orange dress, sparkling and sparkling and sparkling in the sunlight...

8

Lying on the Carpet with Lisa

Lisa held out the orange sequined dress. "I finished it!" she said.

It was the next Saturday and back in Lisa's bedroom she and Dennis had been poring over every page of the new issue of *Vogue*, before she surprised him.

The dress was perfect.

"That is the most beautiful thing," said Dennis, "that I've ever seen."

"Why, thank you, Dennis!" Lisa laughed a little, slightly embarrassed by the weight of the compliment. "Actually, I want you to have it. It's a present."

"For *me*?" asked Dennis.

"Yes, Dennis, you love it so much. You should have it."

"I couldn't…"

"Yes, you could."

She handed him the dress.

"Er, thanks Lisa," said Dennis, taking it from her. It was heavier than he imagined, and the sequins felt unlike anything he had felt before. It was a work of art. Quite simply the best present he had ever been given. But where would he keep it? He couldn't exactly hang it next to his anorak in the wardrobe he shared with his brother.

And what was he going to *do* with it?

"Why don't you try it on?" said Lisa.

Dennis's stomach did a flip. He felt how a new companion on *Dr Who* must feel when they're about to enter the Tardis for the first time. Now this really *was* going to be different.

"It'll be fun," said Lisa.

Dennis looked at the dress. It *would* be fun to try it on. "Well… if you're sure."

"I'm sure."

Dennis took a deep breath.

"Just for a moment, though," he said.

"Yay!"

Dennis started to take off his clothes, then suddenly felt really embarrassed.

"Don't worry, I won't look," said Lisa, closing her eyes.

Dennis undressed down to his socks and pants, and then stepped into the dress and pulled it up over his shoulders. It felt different to wearing his normal boy's clothes. The fabric felt so unfamiliar next to his skin – all silky and smooth. He reached around for the zip at the back.

"I'm not sure I can…"

"Let me," said the expert, opening her eyes. "Turn around." She guided the zip up his back. "It looks great. How does it feel?"

"Nice. It feels nice." In fact it felt more than nice; it felt wonderful. "Can I see in the mirror?"

"Not yet. We haven't found the shoes!" Lisa pulled out some stunning high-heeled gold shoes with red soles on the bottom. "I got these in Oxfam. They're Christian Louboutins, but the old dear in the shop only charged me two quid for them!"

Dennis wondered if Christian Louboutin might ever need them back.

He bent down to put the shoes on. "You'd better take your socks off first," Lisa said, looking down at his bedraggled grey socks. His big toe poked out of one particularly large hole.

They *were* rather spoiling the look.

"Oh, yes, of course," said Dennis, before tugging them off, and placing his feet in the narrow shoes. The heels were quite high and he felt for a second that he might topple over. Lisa held his hand to steady him.

"*Now* can I look in the mirror?" he asked.

"You haven't got any make-up on yet."

"No, Lisa, no!"

"You've got to do this properly, Dennis." Lisa reached for her make-up bag. "This is so much fun! I always wanted a little sister. Now, do this with your lips." She stretched her mouth open and he copied her. She rolled the lipstick gently across his lips. It felt weird. Nice, but weird. He never knew lipstick tasted like that – oily and waxy.

"Eye shadow?"

"No I really don't—" protested Dennis.

"Just a little!"

He closed his eyes as she lightly applied some silver eye shadow with a little brush. "Looking good, Dennis," she said. "Or should I say Denise!"

"That's what my brother called me when he found out about the magazine."

"Well, that's your girl's name I suppose. Your *name* is Dennis, but if you were a girl you'd be called Denise."

"Can I look in the mirror yet?" he asked.

Lisa adjusted the dress expertly before silently leading him to the mirror on the

bedroom wall. Dennis gazed at himself. For a moment he was shocked by what he saw. Then the shock turned to wonder, and he laughed. He felt so happy he wanted to dance. Sometimes you feel things so deeply that words aren't enough. He started to move around in front of the mirror. Lisa joined in, humming some made-up music.

For a moment they were in their own crazy little musical, before they fell to the floor laughing.

"I guess you like it then?" asked Lisa, still giggling.

"Yes… it's just a bit…"

"Strange?"

"Yes. A bit strange."

"You look good, though," offered Lisa.

"Really?" said Dennis. He was enjoying lying on the carpet with Lisa a little too much and felt embarrassed, so he got up and looked at himself in the mirror again. Lisa followed him.

"Yeah, in fact you look great," she said. "You know what?"

"What?" asked Dennis eagerly.

"I think you could fool anybody dressed like that. You look just like a girl."

"Really? Are you sure?" Dennis looked at himself again in the mirror, squinting. He tried to imagine that he was looking at a stranger.

He *did* look a bit like a girl...

"Yeah," said Lisa. "I'm sure. You look amazing. Do you want to try on something else?"

"I don't know if I should," said Dennis, suddenly self-conscious. "Someone might come in."

"My mum and dad are at the garden centre. It's so boring but they love it there! Trust me, they won't be back for hours."

"Well, maybe this one then?" said Dennis, displaying a long purple dress that Lisa had copied from one she'd seen Kylie wear at an awards do.

"Nice choice!"

Then he tried on a short red dress that Lisa's mum had bought for her to wear to a family wedding, then a little yellow puff-ball skirt from the 1980s that her Auntie Sue had passed onto her, then a lovely nautical-themed blue and white striped dress that Lisa had found in Cancer Research.

That afternoon, Dennis ended up trying on everything in Lisa's wardrobe. Gold shoes, silver shoes, red shoes, green shoes, boots, big handbags, little handbags, clutch-bags, blouses, long flowing skirts, mini-skirts, earrings, bangles, hair scrunchies, fairy wings, even a tiara!

"It's not fair," said Dennis. "Girls have got all the best stuff!"

"Rules don't apply here," laughed Lisa. "Dennis, you can be whoever you want to be!"

9

Bonjour, Denise

The next morning Dennis was in bed lying perfectly still, but he felt like he was on a rollercoaster. His mind was racing. Dressing up had made him feel like he didn't have to be boring Dennis living his boring life anymore. *I can be whoever I want to be!* he thought.

He took a shower. The bathroom was dark green like an avocado. Dennis had never understood why his parents had chosen such a revolting colour for a bathroom. If he had been consulted he would have installed a white antique bath, which he would have complemented with black and white tiles. But being a child, he'd never been asked for his opinion.

To use the shower you needed the precision of a safe cracker. Turn the dial one millimetre to the left or right and the water would go either ice cold or boiling hot. Dennis positioned the dial exactly where it should be so as not to be frozen or scalded to death, and squeezed some Imperial Leather shower gel on his hand. It was what he did every morning. It was part of the grinding routine of his life. Yet somehow the world was burning with possibilities.

Downstairs in the kitchen, John was eating his toast and chocolate spread and watching the *Hollyoaks* omnibus.

"Dad gone already?" asked Dennis.

"Yeah, I heard him leave at four. Didn't the lorry wake you up?"

"No. Don't think so."

"He said something about having to be up early to take some cat food to Doncaster."

Dennis thought how his dad's life as a lorry driver wasn't as glamorous as it sounded.

And it didn't sound that glamorous to begin with.

Dennis poured himself some Rice Krispies, and just as he was about to eat a spoonful the doorbell rang. It was a confident ring, long and loud.

DRRRRIIIIIIIIIIIIIIIIIIIIING!

Dennis and John were so curious about who it could be at the door on a Sunday morning that they both rushed to open it. The postman didn't come on a Sunday, nor indeed in the morning anymore, preferring to do his round at some hour of his choosing in the afternoon.

It wasn't the postman.

It was Lisa.

"Hi," she said.

"Er…" said John, now suddenly unable to form words.

Dennis knew John fancied Lisa – he stared at her all the time at school. But then *everybody* fancied Lisa. She was so utterly gorgeous that probably even the hearts of squirrels missed a beat when she walked by.

"Um, what do you want?" asked John awkwardly, unable to function properly in this close proximity to beauty.

"I've come to see Dennis," she said.

"Oh," said John. He turned to Dennis with a look of hurt and injustice in his eyes, like a dog about to be put down.

"Come in," said Dennis, loving how much all this was winding John up. "I'm just having breakfast."

Dennis led Lisa into the kitchen. They sat down.

"Oh, I love *Hollyoaks*," said Lisa.

"Yeah, I do too," said Dennis.

John shot him a look that clearly stated, *You filthy liar, you have never previously expressed any interest in the long-running, Chester-based teen soap opera.*

Dennis ignored him. "Do you want anything to eat?" he asked Lisa.

"No, I'm fine. I'd love a cup of tea though."

"Cool," said Dennis, and put some water in the kettle. John gave him another look. This one clearly said, *You never say "cool". I'm so angry I'm going to have to tear off your head and use it as a football.*

"I had fun yesterday," said Lisa.

"Y—yes," said Dennis tentatively, not wanting to give too much away in front of his brother. "I had a great time..." He knew he was driving his brother insane with jealousy so added, "...with you."

"WE ARE MEANT TO BE GOING UP THE PARK TO PLAY FOOTBALL NOW," said John, trying to put emphasis on every word to sound authoritative, but actually only sounding a bit mad.

"You go ahead. I'm gonna chill with Lisa for a while." Dennis looked at John and smiled. Lisa smiled too.

They smiled John out of the room.

Lisa and Dennis listened to the door shutting behind him. Lisa laughed excitedly at all the intrigue.

"Well, how do you feel today?" she asked.

"Well... I just feel... great!" said Dennis.

"I've had an idea," said Lisa. "Crazy, but..."

"Go on."

"Well, you know what I said about how you could fool everyone into thinking you were a girl?"

"Yes..." said Dennis, nervously.

"Well some of the kids at school just had French exchange students staying with them..."

"So?" said Dennis.

"So, I thought... this is crazy but... I thought

I could dress you up as a girl and take you to Raj's and say you were my French pen-pal or something. You wouldn't have to say much, because you know, you'd be French!"

"No!" said Dennis. He felt the exhilaration and fear of somebody who has just been chosen to assassinate a president.

"It could be fun."

"Absolutely not."

"How amazing would it be though? To pass you off as a girl."

"It's insane! I go into Raj's shop every day. He'd know for certain it was me."

"I bet he wouldn't," said Lisa. "I've got a wig my mum bought for a fancy dress party. I could put some make-up on you like yesterday. It'd be so much fun – let's do it today!"

"*Today*?"

"Yeah, it's Sunday so there should be less

people about. I brought a dress with me, 'cos I was hoping you'd say yes."

"I don't know, Lisa. I've got a lot of homework to do."

"I've got you a handbag too..."

Ten minutes later Dennis looked at himself in the hall mirror. He was wearing a short, electric-blue dress and holding a silver clutch-bag. It was a party dress, really, not what anyone would wear on a Sunday morning to a newsagent's shop.

Least of all a twelve-year-old boy.

But having Lisa fuss over him, applying make-up to his face, squeezing his feet into matching silver high-heeled shoes, and styling the wig, had been so much fun he didn't complain.

"Is Raj really going to believe I'm your French pen-pal?" he asked.

"You look amazing. And it's all about confidence. If you believe it, everyone else will too."

"Maybe…"

"Come on, let's see you walk."

Dennis trotted up and down the hall, doing his best impression of a catwalk model.

"Mmm, it's like Bambi taking his first steps," said Lisa with a laugh.

"Thanks a lot."

"Sorry, just joking. Look, you've got to stand upright in heels like these."

Dennis copied Lisa's posture and immediately felt a little more confident in the silver shoes. "I quite like this actually," he said.

"Yes, it's a good feeling, being that little bit taller. And it makes your legs look great."

"Is Denise a French name too?" he asked.

"If you say anything in a French accent it sounds French," said Lisa.

"De-neeze," said Dennis, laughing. "Bonjour, je m'appelle De-neeze."

"Bonjour, Denise. Vous êtes très belle," said Lisa.

"Merci beaucoup, Mademoiselle Lisa."

They both laughed.

"Are you ready?" Lisa asked.

"Ready to…?"

"To go outside."

"No, of course I'm not."

"But?"

"But I will!"

They both laughed again. Lisa opened the door and Dennis stepped out into the sunshine.

10

Pickled Onion Monster Munch

At first Lisa held Dennis's hand to steady him.
After a few paces the tottering calmed down a
little, and Dennis began to walk more easily.

High heels do take a bit of getting used to.
Not that I would know, reader. Someone told
me.

Soon they arrived at Raj's shop. Lisa squeezed
Dennis's hand reassuringly. He took a deep
breath and they went inside.

"A good morning to you, Miss Lisa," said Raj,
smiling broadly. "I have the new copy of Italian
Vogue for you. Oh my word, it's heavy though!

Like a brick! I ordered it in specially for you."

"Wow, thanks so much, Raj," said Lisa.

"And who is your new friend?"

"Oh, this is my French exchange person… student, Denise," said Lisa.

Raj studied Dennis for a moment. Had they fooled him? Dennis mouth was dry with nerves.

"Ah, hello, Denise, welcome to my shop," said Raj. Lisa and Dennis smiled at each other. Dennis looked so good as Denise that Raj clearly didn't suspect a thing. "It is possibly the finest shop of this kind in the whole of England! Now you can get all your postcards to send back home!" Raj picked up a packet of plain white postcards.

"They're blank, Raj," said Lisa.

"Yes, you will have to draw some sights of London on these. I stock an unrivalled selection of felt-tipped pens. So you are from France?"

"Yes," replied Lisa.

"Oui," added Dennis, tentatively.

"I've always wanted to go to France," said Raj. "It's in France, isn't it?"

Lisa and Dennis shared a confused look.

"Well, if there is anything I can do whilst you are in England, Miss... forgive me, what is your name again?" asked Raj.

"De-neeze," replied Dennis.

"It's a lovely accent you have, Miss Denise."

"Merci."

"What did she say?" asked Raj.

"Thank you," said Lisa.

"Oh! Merci, merci," said Raj, delighted at this discovery. "I can speak French now! If there is anything I can do, please let me know. Now, Lisa, before you go, I have some special offers today I would like to tell you about."

Lisa and Dennis both rolled their eyes. "Nine Kinder Eggs for the price of eight."

"No, thanks," said Lisa.

"Non, merci," added Dennis, growing in confidence.

"I have some excellent bags of pickled onion Monster Munch, only slightly out of date. Fifteen bags for the price of thirteen. They are a British delicacy. Your French friend may wish to try them, and take a box home for her loved ones."

"I'll just take the Italian *Vogue* thanks, Raj," said Lisa as she put her money down on the counter. "Goodbye."

"Au revoir," added Dennis.

"Goodbye, ladies, do come back soon."

They left the shop giddy with excitement, running away as they carried the exceptionally heavy magazine between them. Raj came out of the shop holding a box of crisps and shouted, "You drive a hard bargain, Lisa. I'll throw in another box of roast beef Monster Munch absolutely free!"

Raj's voice echoed down the street as Dennis and Lisa ran, breathless with excitement.

11

"These high heels are killing me"

"You did it!" said Lisa, as they sat on a wall to recover their breath.

"He really thought I was a girl!" exclaimed Dennis. "That's the best fun I've had... well ever!"

"Well, let's go into town then! There should be loads of people there!"

"I'd love to Lisa, but these high heels are killing me!" said Dennis.

"Not easy being a girl, is it?" she said.

"No, I had no idea your shoes were so painful. How do you wear them every day?"

He took his shoes off and rubbed his feet. They felt like they'd been put in a vice from the Metalwork room. "Aah, let's just go back, Lisa. I need to get changed and go and meet John up the park anyway. He'll be wondering where I am."

"Oh!" Lisa couldn't hide her disappointment. "Spoilsport."

"Morning, Lisa!"

It was Mac, a boy from Lisa's year. He huffed and puffed his way up the street to join them. Mac was one of the fattest boys in the school, and endured the unwelcome celebrity that went with it. He had been to Raj's shop as he did every day, and was carrying a bag of goodies.

"Oh, hi," said Lisa brightly, before whispering to Dennis, "don't worry, just keep quiet." She raised her voice and said, "So, Mac, have you got anything nice there?"

Unlike most of the pupils, Lisa called Mac by his name, rather than his nickname, "Big Mac and fries". Sometimes children pass on cruelty unthinkingly like they would a cold, but Lisa was different.

"Oh it's just my breakfast, Lisa. A couple of bags of Maltesers, a Toblerone, a Bounty, Jelly Tots, some Skips, seven bags of Monster Munch, Raj was doing a special offer on those, a box of Creme Eggs, and a can of Diet Coke."

"*Diet* Coke?" asked Lisa.

"Yeah, I'm trying to lose some weight," said Mac without irony.

"Well, good luck with that," said Lisa, *almost* without irony. "You know it wouldn't do if we were all thin you know."

"Maybe not. Who's your lovely friend then?" he asked with a smile, as he popped a whole Creme Egg in his mouth.

"Oh, this is my French pen-pal, Denise. She's staying with me for a bit."

Dennis smiled at Mac uncertainly. Mac stared at him and kept chewing. It was quite a long time before he had demolished enough of the Creme Egg in his mouth to resume speaking. "Bonjour, Denise," he mumbled through the chocolate.

"Bonjour, Mac," replied Dennis, praying the conversation wouldn't continue past the few French words he knew.

"Parlez-vous Anglais?" Mac asked.

"Oui, I mean, yes, a little," said Dennis awkwardly.

"I had a French pen-pal come to stay once. Hervé was his name. Nice guy. Smelled a bit though. He wouldn't take a shower so in the end we had to hose him down at the end of the garden." He was still chewing. "Hervé came into school with me, are you coming in with Lisa tomorrow? I do hope so. I think French girls are gorgeous." As he said this a little spittle of chocolate egg ran down his chin. Dennis looked at Lisa with panic in his eyes.

"Erm yes, of course Denise is coming in with me tomorrow," said Lisa.

"I am?" said Dennis, so shocked he nearly lost his lady voice and his French accent all at once.

"Yes, of course you are. We'll see you tomorrow, Mac."

"OK girls, au revoir!" said Mac, before he made his way down the street, joyfully swinging his bag of confectionary as he went.

"Oh no!" said Dennis.

"Oh yes!" said Lisa.

"Are you out of your mind?"

"Come on, at least think about it. What if you could fool everyone at school? It would be such a laugh, and it would be our little secret."

"Well, I suppose it *would* be the most amazing thing," said Dennis, a smile broadening across his face. "If the teachers, my friends, my brother, if everyone believed I was a girl…"

"Well…?"

"OK, but I'm gonna need some different shoes!"

But little did Dennis know, as he tottered home in his uncomfortable shoes, that he was about to take a tumble…

12

Another World

"I'm still worried about these shoes," said Dennis.

"They're fine. You can't even tell they're extra wides."

It was Monday morning, and Lisa and Dennis stood outside the school gates. Dennis was dressed as Denise again, in the orange dress he loved so much. Maybe it was the sequins, or maybe it was his nerves, but he was sweating.

"I can't do it..." said Dennis.

"It'll be *fine*," assured Lisa in hushed tones, as pupils and teachers made their way in to school.

"You won't have to say much. No one here can speak French. They can barely speak English."

Dennis was too tense to laugh at Lisa's joke. "Fooling Raj and Mac was one thing, but the whole school? I mean, someone's bound to recognise me..."

"They won't. You look so different. No one in a million years is going to think you're Dennis."

"Not so loud!"

"Sorry. Look, trust me, no one's going to have a clue as to who you are. But you know, we could just go home instead…"

Dennis thought for a moment. "No. That would be the boring thing to do."

Lisa simply smiled. Dennis smiled back and sashayed into the playground. Lisa had to quicken her pace.

"Calm down," said Lisa. "You're a French

exchange student, not a supermodel."

"Sorry – I mean, desolée."

Some of the kids stopped and stared. The boys always stared at Lisa anyway because she was so wildly attractive. And the girls liked to check out what she was wearing, even the jealous ones who invented reasons not to like her. But now she was with this new girl not wearing school uniform, there was even more reason to look. Dennis could sense all those eyes on him, and loved it. He spotted Darvesh waiting for him outside the classroom as he always did. Sometimes they would have a quick kick-about before the bell rung. Darvesh scrutinised Dennis for a moment, then looked away. *Wow*, thought Dennis. *Even my best friend doesn't recognise me.*

Lisa's classroom was on the top floor of the main school building. Although John was in the same year as Lisa, he wasn't in the same class. And kids two years older than Dennis didn't know him, just as he didn't know them, so Dennis had never met most of the people in Lisa's class. In a school of nearly a thousand pupils, it was very easy to feel anonymous.

Unless, of course, you were unutterably gorgeous like Lisa, or had once put your willy in a test-tube in the middle of a chemistry lesson, like Rory Malone.

By the time they reached the classroom, the bell had already rung. They entered just as Lisa's form teacher Miss Bresslaw was calling the register. Miss Bresslaw was a well-liked P.E. teacher, even though she had quite bad breath. It was school legend that her breath had once broken a window in the staff room, but only the new kids tended to believe it.

"Steve Connor."

"Here."

"Mac Cribbins."

"Here."

"Louise Dale."

"Yep."

"Lorna Douglas."

"Here."

"And Lisa James… you are late."

"Sorry, Miss."

"Who is this with you?" asked the teacher.

"It's my French exchange student, Miss. Denise."

"I wasn't told anything about this," said Miss Bresslaw.

"Oh, were you not? Sorry. I did clear it with Hawtrey."

"Mr Hawtrey, Lisa," chided Miss Bresslaw.

"Sorry, Mr Hawtrey, the headmaster bloke. I cleared it with him."

Miss Bresslaw rose from her chair, and approached the new arrival. As she scrutinised Dennis, she breathed over him slightly. *Mmm, that does smell bad,* thought Dennis. A sort of mixture of cigarettes, coffee and poo. He held his breath. He could feel himself sweating profusely now. He feared his make-up was going to melt and start collecting in a puddle on the floor. There was silence for a moment. Lisa smiled. Miss Bresslaw smiled back, finally.

"Well, that's fine then," she said. "Denise, please take a seat. Welcome to the school."

"Merci beaucoup," said Dennis. He and Lisa sat down together. Miss Bresslaw continued to read out the register.

Lisa reached for Dennis's hand under the desk. She squeezed it softly to say, *Don't worry*. Dennis held onto her hand and squeezed it back, just because it felt nice.

As they made their way down the corridor to Lisa's history class, Mac huffed and puffed his way to catch up with them. "Hi, girls."

"Oh hi, Mac," said Lisa. "How's the diet coming along?"

"Slowly," said Mac, as he unwrapped a Twix.

"Bonjour, Denise," Mac offered nervously.

"Bonjour again, Mac," replied Dennis.

"Ummm… I was just, you'll probably say no, but if you weren't doing anything after school with Lisa, I was wondering if you might like to come and get an ice cream or two with me."

Dennis looked at Lisa with panic. Lisa took over. "You know what, Mac, Denise and I have already made plans for after school. But I know she'd really love to. Maybe next time she's over, OK?"

Mac looked disappointed, but not heartbroken. Dennis was impressed by how tactfully Lisa had turned him down on his behalf.

"Maybe I'll see you again later, then," said Mac. He smiled shyly and overtook them, munching on his Twix and unwrapping a Walnut Whip as he went.

Lisa waited until he was out of earshot before saying, "He really fancies you."

"Oh no!" said Dennis.

"Don't worry, it's cool," said Lisa. "It's great, in fact. It must mean you're very convincing as a girl," she laughed.

"That's not funny."

"Yes, it is," she replied and laughed again.

The first lesson of the day, geography, passed without incident. Though Dennis didn't think his new-found knowledge of Oxbow lakes would ever be of use in the adult world.

Unless of course he wanted to be a geography teacher.

He got away with it in the second lesson too, physics. Magnets and iron filings. Fascinating! Dennis hadn't understood this subject as a boy, and understood it even less as a girl. He was quickly learning that:

It was best to remain silent in class,

Remember to cross your legs when you are wearing a dress, and most importantly,

Don't catch the boys' eyes as you might be more attractive than you thought!

The bell rang again not a moment too soon. It was break-time.

"I need to go to the loo," said Dennis, with a sense of urgency.

"I do too," said Lisa. "Let's go together." Lisa took Dennis's hand and they went through the doors of the girls' toilet.

And into another world…

Boys treated the "boys' room" as a purely functional place. You did what you needed to do, maybe wrote something rude about Mr Hawtrey on the toilet door, and then you left. Inside the girls' room, it was like a party.

It was rammed.

Dozens of girls competed for space around the mirrors, while others chatted to their neighbours in the next cubicles.

Lisa and Dennis joined a queue for one of the toilets. Dennis wasn't used to queuing but found that he loved it. Listening to all the girls chatter to each other and then bustle around each other seemed so new. Without the presence of boys, girls seemed to behave so differently. They talked and laughed and shared everything.

The giggles, the glitter, the glamorous make-up... what a perfect world it was!

Lisa touched up her lipstick. She was about to put her make-up bag away when she paused.

"Do you want me to do yours too?" she asked.

"Oh, yes, please," said Dennis in his best French accent.

"Let me see," said Lisa, reaching into her bag.

"Maybe we should try a different lipstick colour?"

"I've got a lovely pink one here, Lisa," chirped one of the girls.

"I just bought this new eye shadow," said another. Before Dennis could say anything, all these girls were fussing around him, helping to apply lip liner, foundation, blusher, eye liner, mascara, lipstick... everything.

Dennis hadn't been so happy in years. All these girls chatting to him, making him feel special. He was in heaven.

13

Double French

"This is hell," whispered Dennis.

"Shush," said Lisa.

"You didn't tell me you had *French* today."

"I forgot."

"You *forgot*?" said Dennis.

"Shush. And actually, it's double French."

"*Double* French?"

"Bonjour, la classe," said Miss Windsor loudly as she entered. Dennis prayed she wouldn't recognise him from the detention.

"Bonjour Mademoiselle Windsor," said the class in unison. Miss Windsor always started the

classes in French. It gave the false impression that the pupils were all fluent French speakers. Suddenly, she spotted the girl in the orange dress and all the make-up. Miss Windsor couldn't fail to notice her, really. She stood out like a disco-ball in the gloom of the classroom.

"Et qui êtes-vous?" she enquired. Dennis sat frozen with fear, with a terrible feeling he was about to throw up or pee, or both

simultaneously, if that was at all possible.

Frustrated by the lack of response, Miss Windsor abandoned the French speaking, as she usually had to within a few seconds of entering the classroom, and continued in English. "Who are you?" she repeated.

Still Dennis sat in silence.

Everyone looked at Lisa. She gulped. "She's my German pen-pal, Miss," she said.

"I thought you said she was French," said Mac innocently, his voice slightly muffled by the Rolo he was chewing.

"Oh, yes, sorry. French pen-pal. *Thanks*, Mac," said Lisa pointedly. She shot him an angry look and he frowned, looking hurt and baffled.

Miss Windsor's face instantly glowed with joy. She hadn't smiled so much since winning her campaign for the school canteen to serve baguettes at lunchtime.

"Ah, mais soyez la bienvenue! Quel grand plaisir de vous accueillir dans notre humble salle de classe! C'est tout simplement merveilleux! J'ai tant de questions à vous poser. De quelle région de la France venez-vous? Comment sont les écoles là-bas? Quel est votre passe-temps favori? Que font vos parents dans la vie? S'il-vous-plaît, venez au tableau et décrivez votre vie en France pour que nous puissions tous en bénéficier. Ces élèves pourraient tirer grand profit d'un entretien avec une vraie Française telle que vous! Mais rendez-moi un service, ne me corrigez pas devant eux!"

Like everyone in the class, and indeed like most people reading this book except for the exceptionally clever or French ones, Dennis had absolutely no idea what Miss Windsor was going on about. I don't know either – I had to get a friend who had passed their French GCSE to translate it for me. Basically, though, Miss Windsor is delighted to have a real French person in her class and is asking lots of questions about life in France. I hope so anyway, unless my friend is playing a horrible joke on me and Miss Windsor is talking about her favourite episodes of *Spongebob Squarepants* or something.

"Er... oui," said Dennis, hoping that by simply saying yes, he couldn't get himself into too much trouble. Unfortunately, Miss Windsor became even more animated, and led Dennis up to the front of the class, still declaiming excitedly in French.

"Oui, c'est vraiment merveilleux. On devrait faire cela tous les jours! Faire venir des élèves dont le français est la langue maternelle! Ce sont les jours comme celui-ci que je me souviens pourquoi j'ai voulu devenir prof. S'il-vous-plaît, racontez-nous vos premières impressions de l'Angleterre."

Dennis stood still in front of everyone. Lisa looked like she wanted to shout out and help, but couldn't make a sound.

Dennis felt as if he was underwater or in a dream. He looked out into the eerie stillness of the room. Everyone stared at him. Nothing moved except Mac's jaw.

Rolos are extremely chewy.

"May I speak in English one moment?" asked Dennis in a tentative French accent.

Miss Windsor looked a little surprised and a lot disappointed. "Yes, of course."

"Errrm, 'ow can I put this, how you say… politely?"

"Poliment, oui."

"Madame Windsor," continued Dennis, "your French accent is very poor and I am very sorry but I cannot understand anything you are saying."

Some of the pupils laughed cruelly. A single tear appeared in Miss Windsor's eye and rolled down her cheek.

"Are you all right, Miss? Do you need a tissue?" asked Lisa, before shooting Dennis a furious look.

"No, no, I'm perfectly fine, thank you, Lisa.

I've just got something in my eye, that's all."

Miss Windsor stood there swaying like she had been shot, but hadn't quite fallen to the floor yet. "Um, why don't you all get on with some private reading. I just need to step outside to get some air for a moment." She tottered uncertainly out of the classroom, as if the bullet was slowly making its way to her heart. She closed the door behind her. For a moment there was silence. Then from outside the classroom they heard a huge wail.

"Aaaaaaaaaaaaaaaaaaaaaaaaaaaaaaaah."

Then silence again.

Another wail. "Aaaaaaaaaaaaaaaaaaaah."

A little more silence and then an even longer one. "Aaaaaaaaaaaaaaaaaaaaaaaaaaaaaaaaaaa aaaaaaaaaaaaaaaaaaaaaaaaaaaaaaaaaaaaaaaa aaaaaaaaaaaaaaaaaaaaaaaaaaaaaaaaaaaaa aaaaaaaaaaaaaaaaaaaaaaaaaaaaaaaaaaaaaaaaaa

aaaaaaaaaaaaaaaaaaaaaaaaaaaaaaaaaaaaa

aaaaaaaaaaaaaaaaaaaaaaaaaaaaaaaaaaaaaaaaaaa

aaaaaaaaaaaaaaaaaaaaaaaaaaaaaaaaaaaaaaaa

aaaaaaaaaaaaaaaaaaaaaaaaaaaaaaaaaaaaaaaaa

aaaaaaaaaaaaaaaaaaaaaaaaaaaaaaaaaaaaaaaaa

aaaaaaaaaaaaaaaaaaaaaaaaaaaaaaaaaaaaaaaaaa

aaaaaaaaaaaaaaaaaaaaaaaaaaaaaaaaaaaaaaa

aaaaaaaaaaaaaaaaaaaaaaaaaaaaaaaaaaaaaa

aaaaaaaaaaaaaaaaaaaaaaaaaaaaaaaaaaaaaaaaaaaa

aaaaaaaaaaaaaaaaaaaaaaaaaaaaaaaaaaaaaa

aaaaaaaaaaaaaaaaaaaaaaa
aaaaaaaaaaaaaaaaaaaaaaaaaaaaaa
aaaaaaaaaaaaaaaaaaaaaaaaaaaaaaaaaaaaaaaaaaaa
aaaaaaaaaaaaaaaaaaaaaaaaaaaaaaaaaaaaaaaaaaaa
aaaaaaaaaaaaaaaaaaaaaaaaaaaaaaaaaaaaaaaaaaaa
aaaaaaaaaaaaaaaaaaaaaaaaaaaaaaaaaaaa
aaaaaaaaaaaaaaaaaaaaaaaaaaaaaaaaaaaaa
aaaaaaaaaaaaaaaaaaaaaaaaaaaaaaaaaaaaaaaaaaaa
aaaaaaaaaaaaaaaaaaaaaaaaaaa
aaaaaaaaaaaaaaaaaaaaaaaaaaaaaaaaaaaaaaaaaa
aaaaaaaaaaaaaaaaaaaaaaaaaaaaaaaaa
aaaaaaaaaaaaaaaaaaaaaaaaaaaaaaaaaaaaaaaaaaaaaa
aaaaaaaaaaaaaaaaaaaaaaaaaaaa
aaaaaaaaaaaaaaaaaaaaaaaaaaaaaaaaaaaaaaaaaaaaaa
aaaaaaaaaaaaaaaaaaaaaaaaa
aaaaaaaaaaaaaaaaaaaaaaaaaaaaaa
aaaaaaaaaaaaaaaaaaaaaaaaaaaaaaaaaaaaa
aaaaaaaaaaaaaaaaaaaaaaaaaaaaaaaaaaaah."

The mouths of those pupils who had laughed

now closed tight with regret. Lisa looked at Dennis, who bowed his head. He returned to his seat, scraping his high heels along the floor sorrowfully.

A few more seconds passed like hours, before Miss Windsor returned to the classroom. Her face was red and puffy from crying.

"Right, so, um… right, good… turn to page fifty-eight in your textbooks and answer questions (a), (b) and (c)."

The pupils all began their work, more silent and compliant than they had ever been before.

"Would you like a Rolo, Miss?" ventured Mac. No one was more aware of the momentary comfort chocolate could give in moments of despair.

"No, thank you, Mac. I don't want to spoil my lunch. It's bœuf bourguignon…"

She started crying uncontrollably again.

14

Silence like Snow

"You complete &**%$£%!"

Oops, sorry. I know even though real children do swear, you mustn't have swearing in a children's book. Please forgive me, I really am %$£@$*& sorry.

"You shouldn't swear, Lisa," said Dennis.

"Why not?" Lisa asked angrily.

"Because a teacher might hear you."

"I don't care who hears me," said Lisa. "How could you do that to poor Miss Windsor?"

"I know… I feel so bad…"

"She's probably weeping into her bœuf

bourguignon now," said Lisa as they stepped out into the busy playground. It was lunchtime, and people stood in groups, chatting and laughing, enjoying their hour of partial freedom. Football games were breaking out everywhere – games that Dennis would normally have joined in with, had he not been wearing a wig, make-up and an orange sequined dress.

And high heels.

"Maybe I should go and apologise," said Dennis.

"*Maybe*?" said Lisa. "You have to. Let's go and find her in the dining hall. She should be there, unless she's jumped in the River Seine."

"Oh, don't make me feel any worse."

As they made their way across the playground, a football rolled past them. "Kick it back, love," shouted Darvesh.

Dennis couldn't help it – the urge to kick the ball was too strong.

"Don't be too flash," said Lisa as he ran after the ball. But Dennis couldn't help himself, and chased it aggressively. He stopped it neatly, then took a run up to kick it back to his friend.

But as he kicked the ball his high-heeled shoe flew off, and he toppled backwards.

At that moment his wig slipped back off his head and on to the ground.

Denise became Dennis again.

Time seemed to slow down. There Dennis was, standing in the middle of the playground, in a girl's dress and make-up with one shoe on. Silence spread across the playground like snow. Everyone stopped what they were doing and turned to look at him.

"Dennis...?" asked Darvesh incredulously.

"No, it's Denise," replied Dennis. But the game was up.

Dennis felt like he'd looked at Medusa, that Greek mythological monster who turned people to stone. He couldn't move. He looked at Lisa. Her face was dark with worry. Dennis tried to smile.

Then out of the silence came a laugh.

Then another.

Then another.

Not the kind of laughter that greets something funny, but that cruel, mocking laugh, meant to hurt and humiliate. The laughter became louder and louder and louder, and Dennis felt as if the whole world was laughing at him.

For all eternity.

"Hahahahahahahahahahahahaha Hahahahaha**hahahahahaha**hahahahaha

Hahahahahahahahahahahahahahahah
Hahahahahahahahahahahahahahahaha
hahahaHhahahahahahahahahahahahahah
ahahahahHahahahahahahahahahahahahah
hahahahHahahahahahahahahahah
ahahahahahahahahahHahahahahahahahahahah
ahahahhahahahahahaHahahahahahahahahaha
hahahahahahahahahaHahahahahahahahaha
hahahahahahahahahahahahHahahahaha
hahahahahahahahahahahahahahahahahahah
ahahhahahahahahahahahahahahahahaha

Hahahahahahahahahahahahahahahah
Hahahahahahahahahahahahahahahaha
hahahaHahahahahahahahahahahahahaha
hahahahHahahahahahahahahahahahahahah
hahahahHahahahahahahahahahahahaha
hahahahahahahHahahahahahahahahahahah
ahhahahahahahaHahahahahahahahahahaha
hahahahahahaHahahahahahahahahaha
hahahahahahahahahahHahahahah
ahahahahahahahahahahahahahahahahahaha
hahhhahahahahahahahahahahahaha

haHahahahahahahahahahahahahahah
ahHahahahahahahahahahahahahahaha
hahahahaHhahahahahahahahahahahahah
ahahahahahHahahahahahahahahahahaha
hahhahahahHahahahahahahahaha
hahahahahahahahahahHahahahahahahahah
ahahahahhahahahahahaHahahahahahahaha
hahahahahahahahahahaHahahahahahaha
hahahahahahahahahahahahHahaha
hahahahahahahahahahahahahahahahaha
hahahahhahahahahahahahahahah
ahahahHahahahahahahahahahah
ahahahahHahahahahahahahahahaha
hahahahahahahaHhahahahahahahahahahah
ahahahahahahahHahahahahahahahahaha
hahahahhahahahHahahahaha
hahahahahahahahahahahahahahahHah
ahahahahahahahahahahahhahahahahahaH
ahahahahahahahahahaHahahahahahaha!"

"You, boy," boomed a voice from the school building. The laughter stopped in an instant, as the school looked up. It was Mr Hawtrey, the headmaster with the heart of darkness.

"Me, Sir?" asked Dennis, with a misguided tone of innocence.

"Yes, you. The boy in the dress."

Dennis looked around the playground. But he was the only boy wearing a dress. "Yes, Sir?"

"Come to my office. NOW."

Dennis started to walk slowly towards the school building. Everyone watched him take each uncertain, wobbling step.

Lisa picked up the other shoe. "Dennis…" she called after him.

He turned round.

"I've got your other shoe."

Dennis turned back.

"There's no time for that, boy," bellowed

Mr Hawtrey, his little moustache twitching with rage.

Dennis sighed and click-clacked his way to the headmaster's office.

Everything in the office was black, or very dark brown. Leather volumes of school records lined the shelves, along with some old black and white photographs of previous headmasters, whose stern expressions made Mr Hawtrey look almost human. Dennis had never been in this room before. But then it wasn't a room you ever wanted to visit. Seeing inside meant only one thing.

YOU WERE IN DEEP POO.

"Are you deranged, boy?"

"No, Sir."

"Then why are you wearing an orange sequined dress?"

"I don't know, Sir."

"You don't know?"

"No, Sir."

Mr Hawtrey leaned forward. "Is that *lipstick*?"

Dennis wanted to cry. But even though Mr Hawtrey could see a tear welling up in Dennis's eye, he continued his assault.

"Dressing up like that in make-up and high heels. It's disgusting."

"Sorry, Sir."

A tear rolled down Dennis's cheek. He caught it with his tongue. That bitter taste again. He hated that taste.

"I hope you are utterly ashamed of yourself," continued Mr Hawtrey. "Are you ashamed of yourself?"

Dennis hadn't felt ashamed of himself before. But he did now.

"Yes, Sir."

"I can't hear you, boy."

"YES, SIR." Dennis looked down for a moment. Mr Hawtrey had black fire in his eyes and it was hard to keep looking at him. "I am really sorry."

"It's too late for that, boy. You've been skiving off your lessons, upsetting teachers. You're a disgrace. I am not having a degenerate like you in my school."

"But, Sir…"

"You are expelled."

"But what about the cup final on Saturday, Sir? I have to play!"

"There will be no more football for you, boy."

"Please Sir! I'm begging you…"

"I said, 'YOU ARE EXPELLED!' You must leave the school premises immediately."

15

There Was Nothing More to Say

"Expelled?"

"Yes, Dad."

"EXPELLED?"

"Yes."

"What on earth for?"

Dennis and his dad were sitting in the lounge. It was 5pm and Dennis had washed the make-up from his face and changed back into his own clothes. He'd hoped this might at least soften the blow.

He'd been wrong.

"Well..." Dennis wasn't sure he could find

the words. He wasn't sure if he could ever find the words.

"HE WENT TO SCHOOL DRESSED UP AS A GIRL!" shouted John, pointing at Dennis as if he was an alien who had momentarily fooled everyone by taking human form. He had clearly been listening at the door.

"You got dressed up as a girl?" asked Dad.

"Yes," replied Dennis.

"Have you done this before?"

"A couple of times."

"A couple of times! Do you *like* dressing up as a girl?" Dad had a look of distress in his eyes that Dennis hadn't seen since his mum left.

"A bit."

"Well either you do or you don't."

Deep breath.

"Well, yes, Dad. I do. It's just… fun."

"What have I done to deserve this? My son likes wearing dresses!"

"*I* don't, Dad," said John, eager to score a point. "I've never put on a dress, not even as a joke, and I never will."

"Thanks, John," said Dad.

"That's OK, Dad. Can I go to the freezer and have a Magnum?"

"Yes," said Dad, distracted. "You can have a Magnum."

"Thanks, Dad," said John, glowing with pride as if he had just been given a badge that said "Number One Son" on it.

"That's it. No more watching that show *Small England* or whatever it's called where those two idiots dress up as 'laydees'. It's a bad influence."

"Yes, Dad."

"Now go to your room and do your homework," barked Dad.

"I haven't got any homework. I've been expelled."

"Oh, yes." Dennis's dad thought for a moment. "Well, just go to your room then."

Dennis passed John, who was sitting on the stairs gleefully enjoying his Magnum. He lay on his bed in silence, thinking how everything had been ruined, simply by putting on a dress. Dennis took out the photograph he had saved from the bonfire of him, John and Mum at the beach. It was all he had left now. He gazed at the picture. He would give anything to be on that beach again with ice-cream round his mouth, holding onto his mum's hand. Maybe if he stared long enough into it he would disappear back into that happy scene.

But suddenly the picture was torn out of his hands.

Dad held it up. "What's this?"

"It's just a picture, Dad."

"But I burnt them all. I don't want any reminders of that woman in the house."

"I'm sorry, Dad. It just floated out of the bonfire onto a hedge."

"Well, now it's going in the bin, like your magazine."

"Please, Dad, don't! Let me keep it." Dennis snatched the photograph back.

"How dare you! Give it to me! NOW!" shouted Dad.

Dennis had never seen him so angry. He tentatively handed the picture back.

"Have you got any others?"

"No, Dad. That was the only one, I promise."

"I don't know what to believe anymore. I blame your mother for all this dressing up business anyway. She was always too soft on you."

Dennis was silent. There was nothing more to say. He carried on looking forward. He heard the door slam. An hour went by, or was it a day, or a month, or a year? Dennis wasn't sure any more. The present was somewhere he didn't want to be, and he couldn't see a future.

His life was over – and he was only twelve.

The doorbell rang, and a few moments later Dennis heard Darvesh's voice downstairs. Then his dad's.

"He's not allowed out of his room I'm afraid, Darvesh."

"But I really need to see him, Mr Sims."

"It's not possible I'm afraid. Not today. And if you see that stupid girl Lisa, who John says put him up to this dressing-up thing, tell her to never show her face again."

"Can you tell him I'm still his friend? Whatever's happened. He's still my friend. Can you tell him that?"

"I'm not talking to him at the moment, Darvesh. It's best you go."

Dennis heard the door shut, and then went to the window. He could see Darvesh walking slowly down the drive, his *patka* getting wet in the rain. Darvesh turned back, and caught sight of Dennis up at his bedroom window. He smiled sadly, giving a little wave. Dennis put his hand up to wave back. Then Darvesh disappeared out of sight.

Dennis spent the whole day holed up in his room hiding from his dad.

Just as night fell Dennis heard a quiet tapping on the window. It was Lisa. She was standing on a ladder and trying to talk in as hushed a tone as possible.

"What do *you* want?" asked Dennis.

"I need to speak to you."

"I'm not allowed to speak to you anymore."

"Just let me in for a minute. Please?"

Dennis opened the window and Lisa climbed in. He sat back down on the bed.

"I'm sorry, Dennis. I'm really sorry. I thought it would be fun. I didn't think it would end up like this." She put a hand on his shoulder, stroking his hair. No one had stroked Dennis's hair for years. His mum used to do it every night when she tucked him into bed. Somehow it made him want to cry.

"It's ridiculous, isn't it?" Lisa whispered. "I mean, why are girls allowed to wear dresses and boys aren't? It doesn't make any sense!"

"It's OK, Lisa."

"I mean, *expelled*? It's just not fair. Karl Bates didn't even get expelled for mooning the school inspectors!"

"And I'm going to miss the football final."

"I know, I'm sorry. Look, I never meant all this to happen. It's just crazy. I'm going to get Hawtrey to have you back at the school."

"Lisa…"

"I am. I don't know how yet, but I promise."

Lisa hugged him and kissed him for a moment just shy of his lips. It was a glorious kiss. How could it be anything but glorious? After all, her mouth was shaped like a kiss. "Dennis, I promise."

16

With or Without the Dress

It wasn't until the weekend that Dennis was allowed out of the house. Dad had locked the computer away in a cupboard, and Dennis was forbidden to watch the television so he had missed a number of episodes of *Trisha*.

Finally, on Saturday morning, Dad relented and Dennis was let out for the day. He wanted to go round to Darvesh's flat to wish him luck for the final. On the way he stopped off at Raj's to get something to eat. He only had 13p to spend, as his pocket money had been frozen indefinitely. Raj greeted him as warmly as he always did.

"Ah, my favourite customer!" exclaimed Raj.

"Hi, Raj," said Dennis, mutedly. "Have you got anything for 13p?"

"Erm, let me think. Half a Chomp bar?"

Dennis smiled. It was the first time he had smiled in a week.

"It's nice to see you smile, Dennis. Lisa told me what happened at school. I am very sorry."

"Thanks, Raj."

"I must say you had me fooled though! Very good you looked, Denise! Ha ha! But I mean, being expelled for putting on a dress. It's absurd! You haven't done anything wrong, Dennis. You mustn't be made to feel like you have."

"Thanks, Raj."

"Please help yourself to some free confectionery…"

"Wow thanks…" Dennis's eyes lit up.

"…to the value of 22p."

Watching Darvesh pack his football kit for the final was harder than Dennis had imagined. Not being able to play was the worst part of being expelled.

"I'm gutted you're not in the team today, Dennis," said Darvesh as he sniffed his socks to check they were clean. "You're our star striker."

"You guys will be OK," said Dennis supportively.

"We don't stand a chance without you and you know it. That Hawtrey is so evil, expelling you."

"Well it's done now, isn't it? There's nothing I can do."

"There must be something. It's so unfair. It's only dressing up. It doesn't bother me you know. You're still Dennis, my mate, with or without the dress."

Dennis was really touched, and wanted to hug Darvesh, but being twelve-year-old boys, hugging wasn't really something they did.

"Those high heels must have been uncomfortable though!" said Darvesh.

"They're murder!" said Dennis, laughing.

"Here's your pre-match snack!" said Darvesh's mum as she entered the room, carrying a tray piled high with food.

"What's all this, Mum?" moaned Darvesh.

"I made you a little masala, some rice, dahl, a chapatti, samosas, followed by a Wall's Vienetta..."

"I can't eat all this now, Mum! I'll throw up! The game is in an hour!"

"You need your strength, boy! Doesn't he, Dennis?"

"Well yes..." Dennis hesitated. "I suppose..."

"You tell him, Dennis, he won't listen to me! You know I'm so sad you're not playing today."

"Thanks, it's been a horrible week," replied Dennis.

"You poor boy, expelled just for not wearing the correct school uniform. Darvesh never told me, what exactly *were* you wearing?"

"Erm, it really doesn't matter Mum..." said Darvesh. He attempted to hurry her out of his room.

"No, it's OK," said Dennis. "I don't mind her knowing."

"Knowing what?" asked Darvesh's mum.

"Well," Dennis paused, before continuing in a serious tone. "I went to school wearing an orange sequined dress."

There was silence for a moment.

"Oh, Dennis," she said. "What a terrible thing to do!"

Dennis paled.

"I mean, orange is *really* not your colour Dennis," she continued. "With your light hair you would probably look better in a pastel colour like pink or baby blue."

"Um… thank you," said Dennis.

"My pleasure, you can come to me anytime for style advice. Now come on, Darvesh, eat up. I'll just go and start the car," she said as she left the room.

"Your mum's cool," said Dennis. "I love her!"

"I love her too but she's nuts!" said Darvesh with a laugh. "So are you going to come and watch the game then? Everyone will be there."

"I don't know…"

"I know it will be a bit weird for you, but come with us. It won't be the same without you. We need you there, Dennis, if only to cheer us on. Please?"

"I don't know if I should…" said Dennis.

"Please?"

17

Maudlin Street

Dennis felt sick as the referee's whistle blew for the start of the game. Pupils, parents and teachers were all grouped excitedly around the pitch. Darvesh's mum looked like she was going to explode with excitement. She had elbowed her way to the front of the crowd. "Come on, football!" she kept shouting with joyful anticipation.

Mr Hawtrey was next to Darvesh's mum. He was sitting on a strange contraption that was half walking-stick and half seat. The fact that the headmaster was the only person sitting made him look very important, even if what he was sitting on looked bum-numbingly uncomfortable. Dennis pulled up the hood on his anorak so that Mr Hawtrey wouldn't spot him.

He didn't even go to the school anymore, and the headmaster *still* terrified him.

Dennis was surprised to see Lisa standing in the crowd with Mac. "What are you doing here?" he asked. "I didn't know you liked football."

"Well it *is* the final," said Lisa casually. "I just wanted to come and support like everyone else."

"I feel a bit embarrassed now, Dennis," said Mac tentatively. "Asking you out on a date and everything."

"Oh, don't worry Mac," said Dennis. "I was flattered in a way."

"Well, you did look very pretty as a girl," said Mac.

Lisa burst out laughing.

"Prettier than Lisa?" joked Dennis.

"Oi, watch it you!" said Lisa smiling.

Out of the corner of his eye Dennis saw Miss Windsor making her way across the pitch to take her place in the crowd.

"Have you apologised to Miss Windsor yet, Dennis?" asked Lisa, with a tone that suggested she knew the answer already.

"Erm not yet, Lisa, but I will," squirmed Dennis.

"Dennis!" said Lisa sharply.

"I will."

"You did really upset her," added Mac as he somehow managed to put a whole Caramac into his mouth. "I saw her in Raj's shop yesterday, and she cried when she saw a bottle of Orangina."

"Yeah, all right, I will. I just can't do it right now, can I? Not with Hawtrey sitting right there," said Dennis, concealing himself behind Mac's bulk and turning his attention to the match.

The opposition was Maudlin Street. They had lifted the trophy every year for the last three years. It was a notoriously rough school, and their team played dirty, going in really hard for tackles, elbowing opponents, even once poking a referee in the eye. Dennis's school, or rather ex-school, had never won, and all most people were expecting of them was a heroic defeat. Especially now that their best player had been expelled...

True to form Maudlin Street got off to a strong start, scoring in the first few minutes. One of their team was given the yellow card for administering a Chinese burn to one of the defenders before they scored another goal.

Then another.

Darvesh ran up to Gareth. "We don't stand a chance. We need Dennis!"

"He's expelled, Darvesh. Come on, we can win this without him."

"No we can't. And you know it!"

Gareth ran off after the ball. Another goal from Maudlin Street.

4-0.

This was turning into a massacre.

There was a lull for a moment as Darvesh's mum and Miss Windsor stretchered off one of the school's team. One of the Maudlin Street centre forwards had "accidentally" stamped on his leg. Darvesh shouted at Gareth, "Please Gareth. Do something!"

Gareth sighed and ran over to Mr Hawtrey.

"What do you want, boy? This is a disaster!

You're bringing shame on the school!" snarled the headmaster.

"I'm sorry, Sir. But you expelled our best player. We don't have a chance without Dennis."

"That boy is not playing."

Gareth's face fell. "But Sir, we *need* him."

"I'm not having that dress-wearing disgrace of a boy representing the school."

"Please Sir...?"

"Play on, boy," said Mr Hawtrey, with a dismissive wave of his hand.

Gareth ran back onto the pitch. Within moments he was lying in agony on the wet grass, after one of Maudlin Street's forwards booted the ball straight at his groin. The striker then regained possession of the ball and hammered it into the goal.

5-0.

"You know you should really let the boy play, Mr Headmaster," said Darvesh's mum urgently.

"I'd be grateful if you minded your own business, madam," snapped Mr Hawtrey in reply.

"Come on, Mac," said Lisa bossily. "I need a hand."

"Where are you guys going?" asked Dennis.

"You'll see," replied Lisa with a wink. She marched off across the playing fields with Mac trailing behind.

The Maudlin Street supporters once again howled with delight. Another goal.

6-0.

Dennis closed his eyes. He couldn't watch anymore.

18

A Thousand Smiles

"Where the hell are they?" yelled Mr Hawtrey at no one in particular.

The second half was about to begin, and Maudlin Street were all waiting on the pitch, eager to finish off their demolition job. The school's team was nowhere to be seen. Had they run away?

Then, suddenly, Lisa stepped out of the changing room and held the door open.

First Gareth ran out wearing a gold lamé ball gown...

Then Darvesh followed in a yellow polka dot frock...

Then the defenders were right behind in matching red cocktail dresses…

The rest of the team followed in a variety of outfits from Lisa's wardrobe… And finally Dennis came out of the dressing room – in a pink bridesmaid's dress.

There was a huge cheer from the crowd.
Dennis looked at Lisa and smiled.

"Go get 'em kid!" she said.

As they ran onto the pitch, Mr Hawtrey
bellowed at Gareth.

"WHAT ON EARTH DO YOU THINK
YOU ARE DOING, BOY?"

"You expelled Dennis for wearing a dress. But you can't expel us all, Sir!" he shouted back triumphantly.

All the boys in the team lined up defiantly behind their captain, striking poses like they were dancers in a Madonna video. The crowd went wild.

"THIS IS A DISGRACE!" bellowed Mr Hawtrey. He stormed off, angrily brandishing his walking stick/seat thing.

Gareth smiled at Dennis.

"Come on boys. Let's do it!" said Gareth.

The bemused referee blew his whistle before it fell out of his mouth. Within seconds Dennis had scored a goal. The Maudlin Street team were in shock.

They were still 6-1 down, but Dennis and his team-mates were back in the game.

"Woo!" shouted Darvesh, as he hitched up his skirt and weaved round a defender.

Laughing, Dennis scored again. He was on his way to a hat-trick and he was a hundred times happier than he had ever been. He was doing the two things he loved most at once: playing football and wearing a dress. Then Darvesh scored, sliding across the pitch and adding a large grass stain to his frock as he sneaked the ball past the Maudlin Street goalie.

6-3.

"My boy! My boy in the yellow polka-dot dress has scored!" shouted Darvesh's mum.

They were on fire. Dennis set up a fantastic cross for Gareth, who just had to tap it into the net.

6-4.

Gareth being Gareth celebrated like this goal would be replayed forever on *Match of the Day*, doing three victory laps of the pitch, and hitching up his gold lamé ball gown as he ran. The crowd laughed and cheered. Then another goal followed. And another.

6-6.

Now there were only a few more minutes of the game to play.

One more to go. And they'd have done it.

"Come on, Dennis," shouted Lisa. "You can do it!"

Dennis looked over at her and smiled. *It would be really cool if I scored now,* he thought, *especially in front of Lisa... my future wife.*

But, at that moment, Dennis fell to the ground in pain.

The crowd gasped.

One of the Maudlin Street strikers had nobbled him. Kicked him right in the shin when he didn't even have the ball. Dennis lay there in the mud, holding his leg in agony. The referee had seen nothing.

"He's putting it on, ref!" protested the Maudlin Street boy. The crowd booed.

Dennis was trying really hard not to cry. He opened his eyes, and his vision swam.

Lying there, grass pressing into his cheek, he peered up at the crowd. Through the tears he glimpsed a red-checked jacket that looked very familiar...

And then the red-checked jacket turned into a man...

And then the man shouted, in a deep voice

that was even more familiar.

"OI! WHAT'S GOING ON HERE?"

Dad.

Dennis couldn't believe it. Dad had never come to see him play for the school before, and now here Dennis was, lying on the ground with tears in his eyes wearing a dress. He was going to be in so much trouble...

But Dad looked at Dennis and smiled.

"OI! REF!" he shouted. "That kid kicked my son!"

Dennis rose to his feet, his leg still glowing with pain but a warm feeling spreading through him. He steadied himself. Then smiled back over at Dad.

"You OK?" asked Darvesh.

"Yeah," said Dennis.

"COME ON, SON!" shouted Dennis's dad, really getting into it now. "YOU CAN DO IT!"

"I called him at half-time," said Darvesh. "After what you said about your dad never seeing you play in a match, I thought you wouldn't want him to miss this."

"Thanks, mate," said Dennis. Whenever he thought Darvesh couldn't surprise him any more, couldn't be a better friend, he went ahead and did it.

Gareth tackled the ball off one of the Maudlin Street boys. Darvesh ran up the outside, and

Gareth passed to him. Maudlin Street charged towards Darvesh and he passed back to Gareth. Gareth panicked for a moment, then passed to Dennis, who weaved straight past the defence before booting it right over the goalie's head and into the back of the net.

The keeper didn't stand a chance.

6-7!

The final whistle blew. It was all over.

"Yyyyyyyyyyyyyyyyeeeeeeeeeeeeeeeeeeee eeeeeesssssssssssssssssssssss!" shouted the crowd. "GGGGGGOOOOOOOOONNNNNNN MYYYYYSSSSOOOOONNNNNN!!!" shouted Dennis's dad.

Dennis looked over and smiled. For a moment he thought he saw John's face in the crowd, but he couldn't be sure as everything seemed to blur in all the excitement. Gareth was first to go up and hug Dennis. Darvesh was next. Within moments they were all hugging excitedly, celebrating their victory. The school had never even got to the semis before – and now they'd won the cup!

Dad couldn't contain his excitement and ran on to the pitch. He scooped Dennis up into his arms and sat him on his shoulders.

"This is my son! This is my boy!" shouted Dad, helpless with pride.

The crowd erupted with cheers again. Dennis smiled a thousand smiles. He looked down at Gareth, Darvesh and the rest of the team all wearing their dresses.

There's just one problem, Dennis thought. *I don't feel that different anymore.*

But he kept that thought to himself.

19

Dragged in the Mud

The Maudlin Street team and their supporters stomped off muttering things like "fix", "re-match" and "bunch of woofters!"

Gareth passed the gleaming silver cup to Darvesh to hold.

The crowd cheered.

"My son! My son the footballer! And yellow is *so* your colour!" exclaimed Darvesh's mum. Darvesh looked over at his mum, and held the cup up to her.

"This is for you, Mum," he said.

She pulled out one of her tissues and wiped a

tear from her eye. Darvesh then passed the cup to Dennis. At that moment Mr Hawtrey reappeared.

"NOT YOU, BOY!"

"But, Sir?" implored Dennis.

"You are still expelled from this school."

The crowd started booing. Mac took a toffee bon-bon out of his mouth momentarily and joined in. Even Miss Windsor allowed herself a little French revolutionary boo.

"SILENCE!"

And there was silence. Even the adults were scared.

"But I thought…" said Dennis.

"Whatever you thought, boy, was wrong," snarled Mr Hawtrey. "Now get off the school premises before I call the police."

"But, Sir…"

"NOW!"

Dad waded in.

"You're a right idiot you," he said. Mr Hawtrey was taken aback. No one had spoken to him like that before. "My boy just won the cup for your school."

"My son Darvesh helped too!" added Darvesh's mum.

"Dennis was expelled though," said Mr Hawtrey with a sickeningly smug smile.

"You know what? I've got a good mind to shove that cup up your whatsit!" said Dad.

"Oh dear, he's more embarrassing than me," muttered Darvesh's mum.

"Look, Mr…"

"Sims. And he's Dennis Sims. My son, Dennis Sims. Remember that name. He'll be a famous footballer one day. You mark my words. And I'm his dad, and I couldn't be prouder. Come on, son, let's go home," said Dad, as he took Dennis's hand, and led him home across the pitch.

Dennis's dress dragged in the mud, but he held Dad's hand tightly, as he sloshed through the puddles.

20

Blouse and Skirt

"I'm sorry there's mud all over this," said Dennis as he handed back the bridesmaid dress to Lisa. It was later that afternoon and they were sat on the floor in her bedroom.

"Dennis, I'm sorry. I tried," said Lisa.

"Lisa. You were amazing. Thanks to you I got to play in the final. That's what really mattered. I guess I just need to find another school that might take me – the boy in the dress."

"Maudlin Street maybe?" said Lisa with a smile.

Dennis laughed. They sat in silence for a

moment. "I am going to miss you," he said.

"I'm gonna miss you too, Dennis. It's gonna be sad not seeing you at school, but we can still get together at the weekends can't we?"

"I want to. Thank you for everything, Lisa."

"What have you got to thank me for? I got you expelled!"

Dennis paused.

"Lisa, I want to thank you for opening my eyes."

Lisa looked down, shyly. Dennis had never seen her look like that before.

"Well, thank you, Dennis. That's the loveliest thing anyone has ever said to me."

Dennis smiled, and his confidence grew for a moment.

"And I have to tell you something, Lisa. Something I've wanted to tell you for ages."

"Yes?"

"I am completely, madly…"

"Completely, madly what?"

But he just couldn't say it. Sometimes it's hard to say the things you feel.

"I'll tell you when I'm older."

"Promise, Dennis?"

"I promise."

I hope he does. We all have someone who, when we are near them, our heart feels like it is in the sky. But even when you're a grown-up, sometimes it's hard to say the things you feel.

Lisa ran her hands through Dennis's hair. He shut his eyes, so he could feel it more.

On the way home, Dennis walked past Raj's shop. He wasn't going to stop, but Raj spotted him and came out of the shop to see him.

"Dennis you look so sad! Come in, come in! What on earth is the matter, young man?"

Dennis told him what had happened at the

football match, and Raj shook his head in disbelief.

"You know the irony, Dennis?" proclaimed Raj. "Those people who are so quick to judge, be they teachers or politicians or religious leaders or whatever, are normally up to far worse themselves!"

"Maybe," murmured Dennis, half-listening.

"Not maybe, Dennis. It's true. You know that headmaster of yours, what's his name?'

"Mr Hawtrey."

"That's it. Mr Hawtrey. I could swear there's something strange going on with him."

"Strange?" asked Dennis, intrigued.

"I don't know for sure," continued Raj, "but you see he used to come in here every Sunday morning at 7 o' clock in the morning for his *Telegraph*. Same time every week, on the dot. And then after a while he stopped coming and his sister came instead. At least, he *said* it was his sister."

"What do you mean?"

"Well, I can't put my finger on it, but there's something very peculiar about that woman."

"Really? What?"

"Come tomorrow at 7 o'clock and see for yourself." Raj tapped his nose. "Now, do you want the other half of that Chomp bar? I can't seem to shift it."

"It's very early for a Sunday," complained Lisa. "It's six forty-five. I should be in bed."

"I'm sorry," said Dennis.

"So Hawtrey's got a sister. So what?"

"Well, Raj said there was something funny about her. Look, we'd better hurry up if we want to be there for seven."

They quickened their pace along the cold,

misty streets. The ground was damp from an overnight storm. No one else was up yet, and the absence of people gave the town an eerie feel. Lisa was of course wearing heels, though Dennis wasn't on this particular occasion. All that could be heard was the click-clacking of her heels down the street.

Then, out of the grey mist stepped a very tall woman dressed in black. She entered the shop. Dennis checked his watch.

Seven o'clock precisely.

"That must be her," whispered Dennis. They tiptoed over to the shop window and peered through the glass. This woman was indeed buying a copy of the *Sunday Telegraph*.

"So she's buying a newspaper? So what?" whispered Lisa.

"Shush," shushed Dennis. "We haven't had a proper look at her yet."

Raj spotted Dennis and Lisa through the glass and gave them a big wink as the woman turned around. They retreated behind a bin as she made her way out of the shop. Neither Dennis nor Lisa could believe what they saw. If it was Mr Hawtrey's sister it must have been his twin. She even had a moustache!

The figure looked about to see no one was around and then hurried down the street. Dennis and Lisa looked at each other and smiled.

Gotcha!

"MR HAWTREY!" shouted Dennis.

The figure turned and said in a low, manly voice, "Yes?" before immediately raising its voice for a lady-like tone, "Um, I mean no!"

Dennis and Lisa approached.

"I'm not Mr Hawtrey. No... no... definitely not. I'm his sister Doris."

"Come off it, Mr Hawtrey," said Lisa, "we may be kids but we're not stupid."

"And why have you got a moustache?" accused Dennis.

"I have a very slight facial hair problem!" was the high-pitched reply. Dennis and Lisa just laughed. "Oh, it's you. The boy in the dress," snarled Mr Hawtrey, in a low voice. He knew the game was up now.

"Yes," replied Dennis, "the boy you *expelled* for wearing a dress. And here you are wearing one yourself."

"It's not a dress, boy. It's a blouse and skirt," snapped Mr Hawtrey.

"Nice heels, Sir," said Lisa.

Mr Hawtrey's eyes bulged. "What do you want from me?" he demanded.

"I want Dennis reinstated at the school," demanded Lisa.

"Impossible, I'm afraid. Not wearing the correct school uniform is a very serious offence," said Mr Hawtrey with headmasterly confidence.

"Well, what if it got out that you liked dressing like this?" asked Lisa. "You'd be a laughing stock."

"Are you trying to blackmail me?" Mr Hawtrey asked severely.

"Yes," said Lisa and Dennis simultaneously.

"Oh," said Mr Hawtrey, suddenly deflated. "Well, it seems like I have no choice then. Come back to school on Monday morning. In correct school uniform, boy. But you need to swear that you will never mention this to anyone," added Mr Hawtrey sternly.

"I swear," said Dennis.

Mr Hawtrey looked at Lisa. She was silent for a moment, enjoying the power she still had over him. She smiled wider than a grand piano.

"Oh, OK, I swear too," she said eventually.

"Thank you."

"Oh and another thing I almost forgot," said Dennis.

"Boy?"

"Yeah, let's have proper footballs allowed in the playground at break-time from now on," continued Dennis confidently. "It's no good playing with tennis balls."

"Anything else?" roared Mr Hawtrey.

"No, I think that's everything," said Dennis.

"If we think of anything else we'll let you know," added Lisa.

"Thank you so much," said Mr Hawtrey sarcastically. "You know, it's not always easy being a headmaster. Shouting at people all the time, telling them off, expelling them. I need to dress up like this to unwind."

"Well that's cool, but why don't you try being a bit nicer to everyone?" asked Lisa.

"Utterly absurd idea," replied Mr Hawtrey.

"See you on Monday then, Miss!" said Dennis laughing. "Sorry, I mean, Sir!"

Mr Hawtrey turned and began to run home as fast as his heels would let him. Just as he was about to disappear around the corner, he kicked his shoes off, picked them up and started sprinting.

Dennis and Lisa laughed so loudly they woke up the whole street.

21

Big Hairy Hands

"What are you wearing that for?" asked Dad.

It was Monday morning and he was staring at Dennis, who was sitting at the kitchen table eating his Rice Krispies, and for the first time in a week wearing his school uniform.

"I'm going back to school today, Dad," replied Dennis. "The headmaster has changed his mind about me being expelled."

"He has? Why? He's a nasty piece of work that man."

"It's a long story. I suppose he thought that the dressing up wasn't so bad after all."

"Well, he's right. It isn't. You know I was very proud of you out there on that pitch. You were very brave."

"That boy really did kick me pretty hard," said Dennis.

"I don't just mean that. I mean going out there in a dress. *That* was brave. I wouldn't be able to do it. You're a great lad really, you are. It hasn't been easy for you since your mum left. I've been very unhappy and I know sometimes I've taken it out on you and your brother, and I am sorry for that."

"It's OK, Dad. I still love you."

Dad reached into his jacket pocket and pulled out the photograph he had taken of his family at the beach.

"I didn't have the heart to burn it, son. It's just too painful for me to look at photos like that. I loved your mum very much you see? I still love her now, after everything. Being a grown-up is complicated like that. But it's your photo, Dennis. You keep it safe." Dad's hand trembled as he passed the charred photograph back to his son. Dennis looked at it again, then slid it carefully into his breast pocket.

"Thanks, Dad," he said.

"All right?" said John as he entered the room. "You coming back to school then?"

"Yeah," replied Dennis.

"That stupid headmaster changed his mind," added Dad.

"Well, I think you're very brave going back," said John as he put some stale slices of bread in the toaster. "Some of the older kids might pick on you."

Dennis looked down at the lino.

"Well, you need to look after your brother then, don't you, John?" said Dad.

"Yeah, I will. If anyone has a go, I'll have a go back. You're my brother and I'll protect you."

"Good boy, John," said Dad, trying not to cry. "I've gotta go boys. I've gotta drive a load of bog rolls to Bradford." He walked over to the door, and then turned back for a moment. "I am very proud of you both, you know. Whatever you do, you'll always be my boys.

You're all I've got." He couldn't quite look at them as he spoke, and then he quickly left, shutting the door behind him.

Dennis and John looked at each other. It was as if an ice age had thawed, and the sun was shining for the first time in a million years.

"It's a shame you missed the final," said Dennis as they walked to school together.

"Yeah…" said John. "I just had to, you know, hang around outside the leisure centre with my mates."

"That's funny. I thought for a moment I saw your face in the crowd, but I suppose it must have been someone else."

John coughed. "Well… actually, I sort of *was* there…"

"I knew it!" said Dennis, smiling. "Why didn't you let on?"

"I was going to," spluttered John. "But I just

couldn't run on to the pitch at the end and do all that hugging stuff. I wanted to, honest, but... I dunno. I'm sorry."

"Well, I'm glad you were there, even if you didn't tell me. You don't need to be sorry."

"Thanks. Sorry."

They walked in silence for a moment.

"What I still don't get though," ventured John. "Is why you did it?"

"Did what?"

"Put on that dress in the first place."

"I don't know really," said Dennis, a puzzled look crossing his face. "I suppose because it was fun."

"Fun?" said John.

"Well you know when we were younger and we used to run around the garden pretending to be Daleks or Spiderman or whatever?"

"Yeah."

"It felt like that. Like playing," said Dennis confidently.

"I used to like playing," said John, almost to himself, as they continued down the street.

"What the...?" said John, as he and Dennis entered Raj's shop to find Raj resplendent in a bright green sari.

And wig.

And full make-up.

"Morning, boys!" said Raj in a ridiculously high-pitched voice.

"Morning, Raj," said Dennis.

"Oh no, I'm not Raj," said Raj. "Raj is not here today but he has left me in charge of the shop. I'm his Aunt Indira!"

"Raj, we know it's you," said John.

"Oh dear," said Raj dejected. "I've been up since dawn putting this look together.

What gave it away so quickly?"

'The stubble," said Dennis.

"The Adam's apple," added John.

"Those big hairy hands," continued Dennis.

"All right, all right, I get the point," said Raj hurriedly. "I was hoping I'd get my own back by fooling you, Dennis, after you played that trick on me!"

"Well you very nearly did fool me, Raj," said Dennis kindly. "You were incredibly convincing as a woman." He smiled, looking admiringly at Raj's outfit. "So where did you get the sari?"

"It's my wife's. Luckily she's a very big lady so it's a good fit." Raj lowered his voice for a moment and looked around so no one else could hear. "She doesn't know I've got it on so if you see her it's best not to mention it."

"It's OK, Raj, we won't," said Dennis.

"Thank you so much. Good tip about your headmaster Mr Hawtrey, yes?" said Raj with a wink of his eye-liner caked eye.

"Oh yes, thank you, Raj," said Dennis, winking back.

"What's that about Hawtrey?" asked John.

"Oh nothing. He just likes to read the *Sunday Telegraph* that's all," said Dennis.

"Well, we'd better go, we're gonna be late,"

said John tugging his brother's arm. "Erm just this bag of Quavers, please, Raj."

"Buy two bags of Quavers, I give you one extra one free," said Raj with great delight at his new special offer.

"All right then," said John. "That sounds good." He picked up another bag of Quavers and gave it to Dennis.

Raj then produced a single Quaver from a bag. "And there is your free Quaver. So that's two bags of Quavers... 58p. Thank you so much!"

John looked confused.

"Good luck today, Dennis," exclaimed Raj as the two boys left his shop. "I'll be thinking of you."

22

One Thing Left to Do

Entering the school gates, Dennis spotted Darvesh waiting for him holding a brand new football.

"Do you fancy a kick-about?" asked Darvesh. "My mum bought me this yesterday. We're allowed to play with proper footballs in the playground now," he added, bouncing the ball triumphantly.

"Really?" said Dennis. "I wonder why Hawtrey changed his mind…"

"Do you wanna play then?" asked Darvesh eagerly.

At that moment Dennis saw Miss Windsor parking her yellow Citroen 2CV. It wasn't so much a car, more a dustbin on wheels, but it was French, and she loved it.

"I'll catch up with you at break, OK?" said Dennis.

"OK, Dennis, we'll have a proper game then," replied Darvesh, doing keepie-uppies as he made his way to the classroom.

"John, wait here a moment, will you?" said Dennis. "There's one thing I still need to do."

Dennis took a deep breath. "Miss?" he called out. John hung back a little.

"Oh, it's you," said Miss Windsor frostily. "What do you want?"

"I just wanted to say I'm really sorry. I am. I'm sorry. I really shouldn't have said that you didn't have a good French accent."

Miss Windsor remained silent and Dennis

squirmed, trying to think of something else to say.

"Because you do. You actually have a really good French accent, Miss. Mademoiselle. It sounds like you are actually a proper French person."

"Well thank you, Dennis, or *'merci beaucoup, Dennis'* as I would say in *français*," said Miss Windsor, warming a little. "Well done on Saturday. Wonderful match. You actually looked very convincing in a dress, you know."

"Thank you, Miss."

"Actually, I'm glad you're here," said Miss Windsor. "You see, I've written a play…"

"Oh yes…" said Dennis with trepidation.

"It's a play about the life of Joan of Arc, the fifteenth century French religious martyr…"

"Wow, that sounds… erm."

"None of the girls want to play her. Anyway

I thought it would be fascinating to have a boy play her, as she of course was a girl who wore boy's clothing. Dennis, I think you would make a very memorable Joan."

Dennis looked to his brother for help, but John just smirked.

"Well it certainly sounds... interesting..."

"Wonderful. Let's meet up at break-time and discuss it over a *pain au chocolat*."

"OK, Miss," said Dennis, trying to hide his dread. He walked away slowly and quietly, as you might retreat from a bomb that may be about to go off.

"Oh, I should have said – the play is entirely in French. Au revoir!" she called after him.

"Au revoir," he called back in the most un-French accent he could manage.

"Now *that* I can't wait to see!" said John laughing.

As they walked off together towards the main school building, John put his arm around him. Dennis smiled.

The world felt different.

Thank yous:

I would like to thank my literary agent at Independent Talent, Paul Stevens; Moira Bellas and everyone at MBC PR; all at HarperCollins, especially my publisher Ann-Janine Murtagh and my editor Nick Lake for their belief in the project and tremendous support of me; James Annal, the cover designer; Elorine Grant, interior designer; Michelle Misra, eagle-eyed copy-editor; the other side of my brain that is Matt Lucas; my greatest fan and mum, Kathleen; and my sister Julie for dressing me up in the first place.

Most of all though, I would like to thank the great Quentin Blake, who has brought more to this book than I could have ever dared to dream.